Sometimes There's a Dove

By Cynthia Ward

To Mr. Abadie
Thank you for accepting
me into the Journalism
program!
Cynthia Ward
Weil
1-23-10

Twilight Times Books
Kingsport, Tennessee

Sometimes There's a Dove

This is a work of fiction. All concepts, characters and events portrayed in this book are used fictitiously and any resemblance to real people or events is purely coincidental.

Twilight Times Books
P O Box 3340
Kingsport, TN 37664
www.twilighttimesbooks.com/

First paperback printing, July 2004

Library of Congress Cataloging-in-Publication Data

Ward, Cynthia.
Sometimes there's a dove / Cynthia Ward.
p. cm.
ISBN 1-931201-74-9 (pbk. : alk. paper)
1. Children of sharecroppers--Fiction. 2. World War, 1939-1945--Tennessee--Fiction. 3. Racially mixed children--Fiction. 4. Delta (Miss. : Region)--Fiction. 5. Oak Ridge (Tenn.)--Fiction. 6. Plantation life--Fiction. 7. Indian children--Fiction. 8. Sharecroppers--Fiction. 9. Depressions--Fiction. 10. Mississippi--Fiction. I. Title.

PS3623.A7316S66 2004
813'.6--dc22

2004001582

Printed in the United States of America

This novel is lovingly dedicated to
one of the world's greatest Mothers

Charlene Brewer

Thank you for always being there for all of
us and for giving so much of yourself to
rear us in the Lord with love, health, and
happiness. I praise God that He chose
you to be my Mother.....

All my thanks and praise to The
good Lord above who makes
all things possible....

Contents

Chapter One

From D'Lo to the Delta

SUMMER'S end was nearing in 1939 and the Great Depression, that had attached itself to the world like a giant leech, kept its solid grip. Daddy's search for a decent job seemed to be as fruitless as the fig tree that Jesus smote.

We left our small town of D'Lo and went to the Delta lands of Mississippi to be sharecroppers on a large plantation where, according to the ad, "The More Children the Better."

There were four of us half-breeds. At least that's what Grandpa says we are. He pure hates the fact that his daughter up and married the son of a Mississippi Choctaw squaw. Zeke, my twin brother, said he didn't care how Grandpa felt; he liked being part Indian.

When we pulled up at Grandpa and Grandma's, Grandpa was standing on the porch. I knew he was itching to plow into Daddy's ears with his opinions. He strolled to the wagon and propped his arm on the side. He glared at Daddy, "Well Cooper, I see ya got cha' teepee and papooses all loaded up and raring to go again. Injun-gypsy, that's what. Dragging my daughter and grandchildren around from pillar to post. Never staying in one place long enough for the dust to settle behind you. Hopping from here to there, always looking for that pot of gold at some rainbow's end. When you gonna stay put? You need to stay put. Get a real job and take care of your responsibility."

"Hey now. Wait a minute, Mr. Claude, sir. That's exactly what I'm doing. Going to provide for my family. There's nothing around these parts and we both know it. I'm not satisfied with hoecakes and sorghum molasses. I have to go where I can get work to provide for us all."

"You have never provided Madge and the young'uns with anything but rambling and poverty. Darn well plenty of that. Just go ahead and admit it. Wandering is in your blood. You just gotta hitch up ever so often and go chasing after the wind. Always looking for what ain't there. Just itching to satisfy your wanderlust."

I knew what wonderlust was and I knew that I had it too. Just like Daddy, I craved the quest for a better life. A life of peace and plenty. Here in Simpson County Mississippi, every day was another battle just to exist.

Grandma came out of the barn, where she'd been milking the cow. She stood beside Grandpa with her hands resting in her stained apron pockets. She reached out and put her gentle fingers against his arm.

"It's their young'uns. Their lives. Their choice, Claude. Let our goodbyes be pleasant. The young'uns are listening to you carrying on like this. It's no telling when we'll see them again. You knew his mind was made up before he got here. Nothing we say will stop this move no matter how much huffing and puffing is done."

"Well now, Jennie. Young'uns need stability. They depend on something staying the same. Where is any stability in such a gallivanting lifestyle?"

Daddy smiled down at them. "Well now, here's some stability for you. We can all count on me for gallivanting."

Daddy bowed his head and checked the reins. He yelled for Old Dolly, our mule, to "gad-up." We waved goodbye as we watched our grandparents fade into the distance. I began hoping to see that elusive white Dove that Mother says brings all good things.

I had never seen a white Dove in my life. I knew if I ever saw one, everything would be perfect in my world.

We jostled away, all poked down in the wagon bed of belongings. Zeke leaned toward me and whispered. "Hey, Clair. Did you hear Grandpa call us papooses?" He giggled.

"Yeah, what is that anyway?"

"I don't know, but it sounds bad."

"Its not bad." Shelly spoke up. "A papoose is an Indian baby."

"Well, the way Grandpa said it made it sound bad." I squirmed. Mother's cast-iron cook stove was hard against my back. I had no extra room. My spot was better than poor Zeke's. His space was so tight that he had to wriggle in and out like a worm from an apple. We were born two minutes apart, me first. I figured that made me his older sister, even though we were both six. Shelly, the eldest one of us was seven years old. She'd taken her seat directly behind the wagon bench where a tiny bit of shade blocked the early morning sun. It was beginning to rise from the trees and climb into the cloudless blue sky. Bay, who was the baby of the family was four years old. He sat between Mother and Daddy with his head resting on Mother's lap. He'd occasionally pop up and happily inform us of things that were ahead. We were anxious to see what the next curve in the road would bring.

A slight breeze stirred across the slow moving wagon. Mother and Daddy were talking. The rocking rhythm of the wagon, along with the wheels crunching over the gravel, created a lull. It soon put us to sleep. We had been rousted before daybreak and were easily put into napping. The next thing we knew, Daddy was standing beside the wagon with cold coca-colas in his hands.

"Y'all gonna sleep all day?" He shook me. "Don't y'all want to get up and have a cool drink and see this part of the country?" I tried to stretch. "Okay, y'all get out awhile and stretch your legs."

We all four leapt out of the wagon. We took our drinks and walked around. There were lots of stores and houses here. Tall shade trees swept the skyline. A long sidewalk spanned the storefronts.

"Where are we?" Shelly asked.

"We're in Copiah County at Crystal Springs. This is where I think your Indian Grandma was born."

"You don't know because she was left without her Mama, huh?" Zeke said.

"That's right Zeke. Nobody knows for sure. Our families were scattered to the wind. That makes family history pretty hard to come by. They were killed and imprisoned on reservations."

Talking about this usually got Daddy's dander up. Zeke liked to prod him along. He liked hearing about it. He liked anything that had to do with him being part Indian, but it made me sad. Daddy went on telling about the massacres. The forced moves. The broken treaties.

Mother noticed tears beginning to fill my eyes. "Well, I think that's about enough history for one day, Daddy." She glared at him. "Now let's get some road behind us so we can rest at lunch time."

"Everybody limbered up and ready to get started again?" Daddy said as he climbed in the wagon.

We wedged ourselves back into our places. The wagon pressed onward toward our new life in the Delta. We began talking about the riches and fine foods that awaited us.

"If we can get money for filling a sack with cotton, I know I can pick the field clean by myself," I said.

Zeke smiled from ear to ear. "We're going to be rich. After all, there are six of us to pick it."

"Yeah, all of us together. We'll be millionaires in no time."

I hoped there would be enough for everyone.

"Don't start counting your chickens before they hatch now," Daddy said.

"Oh, let them dream. It can't hurt nothing." Mother looked back and smiled at us as the wagon rattled along.

We kept sharing our hopes and dreams, each a little bigger and better than the last. It became a competition to see which one of us could tell the best dream.

The sun grew hot. Its scorching rays beat down on us. It heated any air we may have gotten. Passing cars sent billowing clouds of thick, choking dust swirling around us. We'd duck and try to hide our faces from the suffocating powder. We called it "tire wind" or "car clog." We were starving for a bit of moisture on our parched throats and grumbled. We wondered exactly what a darn *sharecropper* was anyway. Around noon we came to a small row of stores.

"We need to stop here and get something to eat," Mother said. "The kids are tired and hungry. We could find a cool restful place and have a picnic."

"Oh good, a picnic." We all began talking at once. "We could get out of these papoose holes!" Zeke yelled. "My papoose legs want to run and leap and stretch."

Everyone laughed at him calling our places "papoose holes" because of what Grandpa had said. Daddy bought bologna, bread, and coca-colas. We found a place for our picnic…a cool area with a running stream. Mother spread a quilt under the shade of a tall water oak. Its limbs danced against the pale blue sky like green feathers. After eating, we ran to the trickling stream and waded in its cool, whispering waters. When the time came for us to go we begged to stay longer.

"We can't spend the day here," Mother said. "We don't want the dark to catch us."

"We have lanterns on the wagon. Let's stay here all day and travel at night. That would be a great idea."

"I know y'all are tired and hot. What if y'all get sopping wet from the stream. That way, riding on the wagon would be nice and cool."

"Yeah!" We all yelled as we plopped down into the cooling waters all at once. We laughed and rolled and splashed until Daddy said we had to go. It felt exciting to travel wet and cool.

That evening, Daddy reined up Old Dolly in front of a rough wood shanty. Saw grooves swirled through its splintery gray boards. It was not beautiful, but sturdy. Daddy said these cabins had been built for slaves. The first Mr. Roberts had kept quite a few.

Now, this place belonged to his grandson. He used these cabins to house sharecroppers. Our small bleak cabin was one among rows of others just like it. They all seemed to fade into the dust. It was as if they and the ground were one. Cabins and cotton loomed before me as far as my eyes could see. The landscape was periodically dotted with a tree. There had hardly been any trees along the winding roadway. It looked as if no drop of rain or moisture had ever touched this drab, vast, naked land of dust…a forever land of cotton fields.

I was shocked to see so much. It seemed to go on and on without an end. Never in my wildest dreams had I thought so much cotton existed anywhere. There certainly would be enough for everyone.

As we pushed the heavy wooden door it screamed from its rusty hinges. It stood open to expose a large boarded room full of spider webs trembling in the corners. The late afternoon sunlight shocked the drab inside. Its brightness came blasting through the wall cracks and dusty windowpanes. A dirt dauber swept through a beam of light turning its shadowed wings a glistening blue violet. Zeke picked it off the wall.

We walked out the back door. Weeds and bitter flowers had grown tall and stemmy.

Mother stood beside the well fanning her face with her apron. She waited for a cool drink as Daddy drew up the well bucket and started pouring the water into a pail. She quickly scooped up a dipperful and began swigging down the cool refreshment. "Oh, I thought I'd die of thirst," she said.

As Daddy finished emptying the water, a dead rat slid down the well bucket. It plopped into the water pail. Mother screamed. She threw the dipper far and wide then went into a fit of gagging and vomiting. Daddy immediately sloshed out the contents of the pail and began drawing more water.

"Someone must have left the cover off," he said. "I'll draw up some more."

"I don't want to drink from a dirty well. Go to a neighbor's and draw up some fresh, clean water." She walked into the cabin with her apron over her mouth, groaning. "And please, do hurry."

"This'll be good enough to clean with I suppose. But yes, we do need clean water to drink. I'll be right back."

He took another water bucket and walked across the way. Before long we saw a big, black woman coming. She pulled herself along with a sweet gum cane. She swayed from side to side, loudly huffing with every step. A little dog bounded along beside her like a fluffy ball of hair.

"Where's your Momma?" Her voice sounded like thunder rolling on the wind.

"She's inside, waiting for some cool, clean water. There was a dead rat in our well. It made Mama sick," I said as I petted the little black dog.

"Oh, that's bad ain't it? My name is Boo. Your Pappy was over yonder getting water and telling me about that nasty critter. He'll be along directly with some good water." Boo walked over and tapped on the misfitten door. Mother opened it. "Miss Brown, I come over to make myself useful. My name is Boo Stokes. Your man says y'all are moving in this here sharecropper's cabin."

"Yes, I'm Madge Brown and that's my tribe of young'uns out there." She pointed at us. "I've just been sitting here praying for the strength to get started unloading the wagon...to begin doing something to this place. I just don't know where to start. It's so drab in here."

"It looks mighty drab at first, but you'll get used to the bare walls. You can make it homey. Sometimes you just gotta look at small things of beauty, but I can promise you it won't be these unfilled chinks." She laughed and poked her cane into a space between the boards to jab out a dauber's nest wedged there. "But you can make a home anywhere. These cabins beat a tarpaper shack or a bridge girder tent."

Daddy came in with the water and we stood in line around the bucket. He looked at Mother. "What do you want me to bring in first?"

She handed the dipper to Shelly. "Well, I guess what I need first is the broom. The sooner I move these blasted spiders out the better."

She seemed to liven up after the cool drink, like a wilted flower after the spring rains. We all tore into working and getting the cabin fixed up. As I went about my work, the little black dog was on my heels like glue.

"Get on outta here stop pestering that child." Boo rebuked it.

"It doesn't bother me." I smiled down at the little creature. "I kind of like it."

"Well, if you want him you can have him. That is if your Momma don't care."

"I don't care if you keep him, just so long as all you kids understand he's an outside dog."

That night we sat around the table enjoying good company, a pot of boiled cabbage, and a skillet of cornbread. Levi, Boo's husband, had brought it over. The coolness of the evening washed away the heat of the long day. Because of Boo and her family we felt at home.

We lay in bed feeling warm and safe. I watched the fireflies dancing about. They poked holes of light in the Delta darkness outside our naked windowpanes. I wasn't altogether sure about this new life, yet welcomed it as I drifted to sleep.

In the morning, right after breakfast, we started our first day of work. Out on the porch six rolled up sacks lay waiting for us. We were excited to start making money. Each of us grabbed a roll and skipped ahead of Mother and Daddy towards the fields. Bay yelled for a sack too but the six-foot roll was too much for him to carry. He unrolled it and dragged it behind him. It got caught on every limb, stick and briar along the way. Every few minutes he'd cry for one of us to untangle his sack.

When we actually entered the fields it was as if we had joined a beehive of workers. There was row upon row of ripe, fluffy cotton, with hundreds of pickers bent and weaving through the stalks. They filled their sacks and hummed. Some sounded happy, some sad. But they each had a song. Children of all ages ran through the rows playing. Some picked cotton. Some were in the cotton houses bouncing and sliding down the freshly picked cotton stacks. Infants and small children rode on their parents' cotton sacks through the field rows.

I threw my sack out, put the strap over my head, and acted like I had done this all my life. I reached out to pick a clump of ripe cotton. A needle-sharp, dry boll stem pierced my hand. I knelt crying as I held my bleeding and stinging hand. A boy passed on the next row and laughed at me for crying. "Baby, baby suck your thumb, wash your face in bubblegum." He sang out.

Maxine Stokes, Boo's daughter, came over, knelt beside me and rubbed my hand.

"Shush, it'll be alright. I get stuck lots." She put her hands out. I saw several prick marks. There were many cuts and scabs from old cuts. "You got to learn how to go around the stuff and pull up like this," she said as she reached around a boll and pulled the cotton out. "Don't try to pick the cotton from the top or the things will stick you bad."

I wiped my eyes and started picking and shoving the stuff into my sack. Bay still played with straightening his. Shelly looked tired and red-faced even before the heat of the day. Zeke reached for the cotton, jerking his hand back and saying "ouch" with every reach.

"You can't help getting stuck at times," Maxine said. "But the more you pick, the tougher your hands get. You'll learn to reach inside the stalks instead of going at it head on."

"How long have you been picking?" Shelly asked.

"I don't rightly remember. I was born here. I been in the fields all my life. I began like Mr. Bay there, just play picking, ya know. But now I pick and gets pay for my weigh-ins."

"When do we weigh-in?"

"Well, when you get a nice big clump in your sack, it'll weigh-in. I usually wait till mine's at least half full."

Every time I thought I had enough, she'd say, "Shake it down." Then she would take her long sack, give it a quick, hard flap several times. The fluffy sack would flatten and leave a clump at the end. So I flopped mine a few good times.

"I thought I had a lot." I looked at my small lump. "I'm not going to shake mine down again."

"It won't weigh-in as much if you don't. Everybody shakes their sacks down. It saves walking all the way to the scale wagon and having the tallyman shake it down. Only that will show you how little bit you got."

"Okay, okay." I continued picking. I hoped for a nice, big weigh-in as I flew into it. I started shaking my sack down after almost every handful.

"You gonna tire yourself out from all that slinging. You better spend more time picking and less time slinging."

"How can you pick and pick and pick and not be tired? It feels like I've been out here a hundred years with this little clump at the end of my sack hardly growing an inch a year."

"Lawd girl, you exaggerating now! My Pappy tells us 'every bush is holding money and every boll is like white gold in your sack'. At least we know where the gold is. You gotta think of all the folks who pan and pan and never earn one cent for their labor. There's always somebody who got it worst than you. Be thankful for what you got."

I still thought only of my plight. I didn't see white gold. I saw hot fluffy wads of cotton, held in finger-gouging bolls of nasty, dry, needle-sharp brown pods. It irked me when Maxine would sing her little rhyme in perfect happiness. She sang as if she were sitting on the shore of a cool flowing stream without a care in the world.

"Pulling and picking, shoving and shaking. Look at all the money I'm making!"

Her little ditty was in sharp contrast to the mournful, wailing songs of the field folks. Some sang about their heartaches. Some sang about their weary bones, while others sang about Gloryland when this life would be over.

My song was more in tune with theirs than with Maxine's. Her little spry mess did nothing for me!

That boy passed by me again. "You still on that same row? You're slower than a retarded snail." He laughed.

"You shush up Floyd Tanner and leave her be. Tend to your own picking." Maxine came to my defense.

"Why don't you just come on over here and make me, you nappy headed gal."

"Just ignore him, Clair. He's always looking for trouble. If he can't find somebody to fuss with he'll fuss at the wind."

Over time I learned the painful art of cotton-picking and the positive art of relationships with every ethnic group in America. We were drawn together in the struggle to survive and become self-sufficient.

Sometimes all the sharecroppers would get together at the big plantation barn for a night of playing and dancing. On these nights, everyone would come with their children for the happy time. Reels from instruments like fiddles, guitars, washtubs, rub boards, saws, harmonicas, jugs, jewsharps or anything else that would make a note, filled the barn and washed over the land.

Sharecroppers worked hard and played hard. Life in the bottoms was a mournful crying of needs. Mothers rocked babies to the buzzing of mosquitoes in summer and the groaning of wind through the unfilled chinks in winter. The cabins were bleak and unadorned, where dreams, like sweat, were washed away with the passing of time.

Smaller children ran naked through the fields and played in the cotton houses where they'd climb, leap, jump and slide down the fluffy stacks. It was easier letting them run naked than trying to keep them changed and their clothes scrubbed out. This would take time away from picking, so only infants and older children wore clothes. These children were only dressed in winter, at church, or at one of the barn dances.

The summers were blistering on this shadeless dusty land. Even the breeze would burn your face, if there ever was one. A lonesome dead feeling hung over the Delta. Winters weren't much better because of the freezing cold weather that no fires seemed to chase away. The best times were spring and autumn, yet there was planting in spring and harvesting in autumn. Obviously, that elusive white Dove was not here.

Sometimes, if we could get away in the afternoon, we'd walk to the old creek bridge on a quiet country lane. We'd stand in the cooling shade. We'd watch the water swirling from underneath its rickety old planks to go whispering forever onward toward that big river. This place was a contrast to its surroundings. It was special to us all. It provided a place to get away, to swim, to fish, or just to sit, listen and think in perfect cool peacefulness. Our first year had gone by and we were seasoned sharecroppers now.

Chapter Two

James Stokes

THE dew-laced morning erupted with the sharp crowing of roosters. They urged chickens from their roosts and folks to their chores. The familiar smell of breakfast cooking filled the cabin. Mother usually woke before the roosters to begin her day. When Daddy awoke they'd spend these precious few moments, with no one else around, talking together. The muffled sounds of their voices were soothing.

We got out of bed and washed our hands and faces. We combed our hair and lined up on the long, wooden bench, behind the kitchen table. We sat patiently and waited for grace to be said and the food to be passed. Mother stood at the corner of the table buttering hot biscuits. She had already milked the cow, strained the milk through the cheesecloth rag, and set the clabbering bowls in the safe for the thick, yellow cream to rise.

I sat there anxious to taste the warm, sweet milk in my glass. I leaned forward and smelled its rich freshness. I was glad we had chopped down all the bitter weeds from the pasture. When the cow ate that plant it would make the milk bitter, then it wouldn't be good for anything but the hog's slop bucket.

"Wait for the blessing, Clair," Mother said.

"I wasn't tasting. I was just smelling it."

I sat back on the bench and listened to Bay counting the biscuits. We didn't know why he counted them, but never a morning went by that he didn't count each and every one.

Daddy was seated at the end of the table. It gave him a view through the house to the road.

Suddenly he pushed his chair back and called out to James Stokes. "Come on in and join us for breakfast. We've got aplenty."

James was Boo and Levi's eighteen-year-old boy. He was passing by our place on his way home from a Saturday night hoedown.

"Don't mind if I do." James came in and sat at the table.

Our cat followed him through the screened door. Tom purred and rubbed against James' pant leg. He reached down and petted the animal as it moved around him like a slithering snake. Tom loudly meowed for more petting.

"James," Mother said, "would you mind putting that crazy cat back outside for me? We're fixing to eat and he bit one of the kids yesterday morning,"

I knew it wasn't the cat's fault. I had been trying to get rid of a piece of smoked sausage by poking it under the table where Tom lay. I had asked for seconds and knew I had to eat it, but I was too full to finish. I held it under the table and kept on wiggling it until Tom saw the tidbit and pounced on it with a vengeance. He got my finger in the chase.

Now, I couldn't defend the cat without telling on myself. I sat there with my head down wishing the whole thing could be forgotten. Mother thought that the cat was acting awful strange by biting into one of us without a cause.

"Bad cat," James said as he got up and walked to the clothespin bag. He took out a pin and clipped it onto the cat's tail.

Tom took off with a loud, screeching yell.

Mother hadn't noticed what James was doing. She figured the cat had gone wild. She dropped her butter knife and crouched over with both hands pent over her head, screaming, "Rabid cat, rabid cat! Get out of his way!"

Tom screeched and sailed around the room. The commotion sounded like the place was full of wild cats. He went upon the walls and circled around them like he was flying. James opened the back door and we watched Tom sail out of sight.

"Stupid cat," James said. "All I did was put a clothespin on his tail and he lit into a squalling fit." James tried not to laugh as the words came quivering past his lips. "I do declare I believe I saw a blue streak behind him though."

"You have scared the pure daylights out of me." Mother's hands shook as she returned to buttering biscuits with fumbling fingers. "Why do you reckon everything you do has to be done with such a flair of outlandishness?"

James did go an extra mile to see that he brought a difference to the normal course of things. He was most always up to something. He'd pick on us and we'd scream. Mother would scold and James would laugh.

Last Friday out in the field, Zeke had said he was awful thirsty. James had looked over the row and asked him how thirsty he was.

'Terrible thirsty. My mouth is as dry as dirt," Zeke had said.

"Boy, that is thirsty!" James shook his head in seeming sympathy. "I've got something for you to drink. That is, if you want it." James smiled his wicked smile. I knew something was up.

Zeke was none the wiser. "Of course I want it," he said.

Then James told him to open his mouth.

"What?" Zeke asked.

"Open your mouth if you want it."

Zeke opened his mouth and James hacked up and pretended he was going to spit into his open mouth. I do believe I yelled louder than Zeke.

"You're so nasty and mean James Stokes!" I'd said while Zeke stood there mortified and near tears.

Then James said, "Well, I asked him if he wanted it, Mrs. Snooty Clair."

We both ran to Mother to tell her what he'd done while he laughed.

James was the one who told us about old Sackety Billy, the Ghost Train and boogers of all kinds. He told us that old Sackety Billy toted off bad children in his croker sack. We had seen Sackety Billy. He would walk along the train tracks picking up pieces of coal. He'd drop these pieces into that big sack that he had slung over his shoulder. We had seen children's knees and feet poking humps out in that bag, so we knew it wasn't just a tale. He was real. We figured the chunks of coal were probably the fire and brimstone pieces used to burn up those bad children.

I never could decide whether I was good or bad and didn't want to take any chances. To be on the safe side, as soon as darkness fell, I would close the shutters tighter than Dick's hatband.

Mother wanted the cool night breeze to blow through the place. She would try to tell me how foolish I was to believe James. She'd tell me, "James is a fibbing piece of splintered wood, draped in clothes. Pure D aggravation walking around on toothpick legs. You don't need to be paying too much attention to what comes out of his mouth. There is no such things as he tells. Even if there were, God is stronger and He loves us. It doesn't matter how good you are. It's how good God is." Then she'd say, "Hush up now and let the shutters stay open, for goodness sake, before we all burn up!"

Daddy and James sat at the breakfast table enjoying Mother's delicious biscuits. They were talking about James' party night crawling into sunrise. Daddy asked him if he reckoned he'd be able to stay awake through the church service.

"Mr. Brown, you must not know a thing about our meetings. Do you honestly think I'd be able to sleep through any one of Brother Tillman's preachings?"

They both laughed and commenced talking about the Monday cane haul and posthole digging. There had to be a new fence line put up. Some cows were getting through the sagging wire despite the yokes on their necks.

As they talked Shelly leaned over and whispered, "Let's go see if Maxine can come to our church with us."

"Alright. I'm done. Let's see if we can go." Then I turned to Daddy. "We've enjoyed our breakfast. May we be excused?"

Daddy raised his hand in consent. "Yes, you may."

Table manners were strictly enforced and observed in our household. If this exact ritual wasn't followed before you left the table, you got a trip to the woodshed. If he didn't answer back, you had to wait until he did…even if you weren't eating. Even if your plate was clean. You didn't move an inch without being excused.

We walked along the road toward the Stokes' cabin. We played our usual game.

Shelly said, "If a woodpecker would peck wood, how much wood would a woodpecker peck?"

We had to make two words match, either rhyme or beginning letters. We took turns naming things like *a pole and a pile, a stick and a stack, a log and a limb, a basket and a board.* We'd reach further, such as *a frame and a floor,* until we could think of nothing more. The winner was the one who could come up with the last example.

I said *a cone and a cord.*

Shelly argued about it. "Those don't make sense. You can't use them, so that means you lose."

"No I don't! A pine cone is made of wood and a cut cord of wood is the same as any stack of wood like you used before."

"Well, I thought you meant a string type of cord, silly."

We passed Fanny May's house and saw Floyd and Toby wrestling in the yard. Toby was Fanny's devilish boy. He couldn't sleep until he'd caused havoc or torment for somebody. Most folks called Toby "Tar Boy" because his skin was so black that he looked like a midnight shadow. He was lost in the darkness. Mean Floyd is Tar Boy's best friend.

Meaner than rabid dogs and as destructive as raging cyclones, they went about knocking down mailboxes, peeing in water wells, throwing rocks at people and animals, and tearing the pretty wings off butterflies. Just last week they'd pulled our clothes off the line and thrown them in the ditch. When Brother Paul asked them to apologize they'd stood there smirking and declaring that they hadn't done any such thing. We told them that we had seen them.

"Well, you saw wrong." Mean Floyd plopped Tar Boy on the head. "You gonna say you're sorry for something you ain't done?"

"Nope, not none of me."

"Me neither!"

And they both ran down the dusty road laughing together.

Fanny May shook her head. "He's just a growing boy."

Marion Tanner, Floyd's Mama, had too many other things to study on. She couldn't be expected to keep up with what Floyd was up to.

When we got to Maxine's she was in the yard with her tin Whitman's candy box on her lap. She kept things like arrowheads, beads, strings, and rags in it. She looked around as we walked over to her pretend chair. It was a sawed off stump that had worn smooth over the years. She smiled. "Hey, can y'all come to church with me? We're having a 'dinner on the ground' day."

"We wanted you to come with us," Shelly said. "What are you doing out here?"

"Fixing my hair." She scooped up a bit of lard from a bucket beside her and swiped it through her hair as she finished braiding the last little clump.

"You put lard in your hair? Why?"

"Helps it to stay pretty. I have to keep my hair greased else it gets all nappy. Then it can't be combed cause it hurts so bad."

"Tangles you mean?" Shelly asked. "Sometimes we get bad ones, and boy howdy, do they hurt!"

"Especially when Mother combs them out."

I cringed as I thought about the time I had fought to get away from a bad hair combing. Mother had held me between her legs and raked that comb through my aching scalp.

"Yeah, like that, but when I grease my hair and plaits it, then I don't get me no nappy hair."

"Can you fix ours too? We don't like nappy old tangles either."

"Well, I gotta put lard on it, or it won't plait up."

We sat on the stump and she sopped our heads full of lard. She commenced plaiting our hair in tight little braids.

James came up and popped her on the head. "Girl, you're gonna get beat with a hickory stick for wasting the lard like that. Mama's gonna skin you alive."

"You're the one who's getting skinned, staying out all night long. Where you been?"

"Mind your own business." James went inside as we admired our lovely hair and thanked Maxine for her work.

On our way home, we discussed this wonderful secret.

"I won't ever stop putting lard in my hair," Shelly said. "And I won't ever have another tangle."

"You sure do look pretty with all those hair rags. Do I look pretty too?"

"Yes, you do, and we can fix each other's hair like this everyday. I watched Maxine and I know how she did it. I'll show you."

Floyd stared as we walked past.

"Yikes! White pick-a-ninnies!" He fell to the ground, rolling and laughing. "Y'all going to the black meeting this morning?"

"Shut your nasty mouth, Floyd!" I yelled back at him as we hurried on home.

When we walked in the house, Mother threw a conniption fit. She flung her hands up and yelled to high heaven. "What on earth have y'all done?"

"You don't like it either?" We patted our braids.

"My stars above, how could you even think of going to church like that? I'll never get all those rags and grease out of your heads before church time. We'll all be late. Do you even care? What possessed you to do such a thing?" She began pulling the ties loose. She told Daddy to put on another kettle of water and go find her more soap. "But I don't think there's enough soap in the whole county to get this grease out."

Her hands flew as she unbraided braids, yanked and pulled out hair ties. We cried and yelled and watched the rag pile grow.

"Ouch, you're messing up our hair. You're tearing up Maxine's tie rags. She'll be mad about that. Why can't we have our hair fixed like this? Maxine worked hard fixing our hair and now you're messing it all up!"

We fussed. Mother snatched out our tie rags and threw them on the floor. The water kettle boiled and Daddy gathered up soap.

We went to bed that night with our heads still tingling from the many head washings. Our hair was brightly shining from all the lard.

Daddy laughed and said to Mother, "Well, there were two halos glowing through the church house today."

"It's not so funny to poor Boo. Listen to her over there still trying to scrape the cornbread out of that dry skillet. She didn't have enough lard to coat it with. All her grease is in the girls' heads."

The huge moon rose over the trees. The soft trembling notes glided on the air as Daddy swept his bow over the fiddle strings in a lullaby.

Chapter Three

The Train

IT was Monday afternoon. We were chopping the last few patches of bitter weeds from the cow's pasture when we heard the train whistle cutting through the countryside. We dropped our hoes and ran to the station to watch the big engine pull in.

Zeke was first to hear its faint echo. He yelled, "Train's coming!"

He dropped his hoe and took off toward our shortcut path to the depot. In time we'd worn a trail through the fences and fields that twisted and turned, rose and fell, broke and bridged over ditches and trickling streams. This beaten path came out just below the station.

It didn't take us long to follow. Our enthusiasm for seeing the train huffing and puffing into Delta station lent wings to our bare feet. Things like stems, roots or sweet gum balls were only small obstacles that rated a mere grunt or a quick ouch. My dress got caught on a briar bush growing into the pathway. I kept running. The sharp barbs latched into the material like some hungry animal and ripped the hem clear across the front. A long dangling strip fell in a loop to my ankles. I quickly stepped through it and kept running.

Shelly held Bay's hand and ran so fast that his legs were flopping around like a ragdoll's. It looked like his feet were making random contact with the ground.

Zeke stayed ahead of us. He skimmed along free and clear with his head held high. His dark hair stood against the wind. None of us stopped until we got to the station.

As we were catching our breath, Zeke turned his foot up and pulled a briar from it. A round bead of blood rose like a tiny red dewdrop.

I cringed. "Didn't that hurt?"

"Of course it hurt." He stomped his foot on the platform. "But I'm not a tender foot. My feet are tougher than wet leather. It's all that

Indian blood in me. I can run barefoot over the sharpest rocks and not even cry because I'm an Indian brave. Well, almost anyway." He poked out his chest tall and proud. "I even have an Indian name!"

We all looked puzzled.

"Zeke isn't an Indian name," Shelly protested.

"My name isn't Zeke anymore. It's Tommy Hawk!"

We laughed.

"And mine is Bow In Hair Row," Shelly said.

I tried to think of a funny one, but all I could come up with was Flint Rock. Bay said we could call him Tote A Pole.

"No, your best name would be Tad A Pole. You're so little you're like a tad pole."

"No, I'm not. I'm big."

"Okay, then. You are a Toad Pole."

The Delta skyline was growing richer toward the west. The late September sun lay over the solemn trees as they outlined the far horizon. A quick breeze sent tiny dust devils scooting along Main Street as we stood waiting for the approaching train.

The station was a busy and exciting place. Folks were busily going here, there, and yonder. We liked getting caught up in the delicious mood. It gave me a feeling of excitement to pretend I might be one of the passengers. I might be traveling to some far away place. A place where there were special things like trolley cars, elevators, electric lights and tall buildings. It would be so thrilling to see such things... things that I had only heard about or read about. Just to be going some place different...away from the forever fields of cotton, corn, tomatoes and peas. Away from pastures of cows, calves, pigs, chickens and those infernal bitter weeds.

I hated chopping those thriving things. There never was an end to them. Our heifer seemed to love that plant. If there was even one in the pasture she would find it. Then her bitter milk went to the hogs. Every few days the pasture got a thorough going over for any new sprouts. Our everlasting punishment for doing anything wrong was to chop the bitterweeds down.

We'd been sent to the pasture this evening for ruining the last tub of water and killing our rooster in the process. To save the chore of drawing up water from the well, we'd set tubs under the eaves to catch the rain water for baths. We'd use the fullest tub and place it back under the eave after we'd finished bathing. Most of the time at least one or more was full enough for baths. There were usually extra tubs of water, unless something happened, like an unusually dry spell, or somebody messed the water up like we had done this morning.

We had seen Brother Paul holding a baptism at the swimming hole and decided to baptize our pet rooster. Shelly and I did the honors. We dunked the fighting rooster under the water several times to make sure he was good and saved. He'd quit squawking and the skin over his eyes stayed down. Our rooster was dead.

We had seen funerals too, so we prepared for the best one any farm creature ever had. We laid our rooster on a plank and carried him to the pasture behind the barn. Zeke toted one end of the board and I toted the other. We walked slowly behind Shelly, leading with her head down and carrying the Holy Bible. I was dragging the shovel. Bay carried a bouquet of bitter weeds. Zeke had a wooden cross that he'd made from tying two sticks together with some of our kite string.

We dug the shallow grave, dumped that rooster in and covered him with dirt. Covered him all over except for his stiff pointed feet. The grave wasn't long enough for them. Shelly stood on a tree root and read the ands, thes and buts out of the Bible while we mourned. Then we put the bitter weeds on top of the mound and stood the cross up. Just before leaving, we walked around the gravesite slowly singing the only song we all four knew, "Jingle Bells."

No matter now, we were going to see the train. It was that connecting link, joining our imagination to reality. Joining our ordinary, mundane, farming lives to that utopian land out there. Out where wonderful adventures existed. A real world. We felt its nearness with the coming of the train. We longed for that other world.

Old man Grey walked by with his pocket watch in his hand. His humped-up shoulders were level with his ears and it looked like his neck was sprouting from his chest. He was churning his toothless mouth and gazing about as he rubbed the face of his watch with his thumb. "Where have you young'uns been lately? I haven't seen y'all in a long while."

Mr. Grey ran the commissary. Since school had been out for the cotton-picking season we had hardly gone to the store. Daddy wouldn't dare let us spend a nickel unless it was some dire emergency. He couldn't wait till we'd earn enough to be free from the tenant farming and get our own place. Sometimes though, we would get two pennies…one for licorice and one for the offering plate.

"Been keeping busy in the fields," Shelly answered.

Mr. Grey had only one good eye and it wasn't real clear. When he looked at something he'd tilt his head to the good eye side and poke his large eyeball down almost on top of it. We sometimes called him "Cyclops" because of a story we had heard. A story about a man named Homer who had been to some place like Mars. He found these one-eyed people that he called Cyclopses.

Mr. Grey didn't seem to mind, but Mother said we shouldn't be so disrespectful. She'd say, "What if one of y'all had to go around with only one eye? How would y'all like it?"

Then, just as sure as rains come and creeks rise, she'd tell us a story about some poor child with only one little eye. How everyone picked on him. Made jokes about him and hurt his feelings. She never did end her stories until we were crying. The tears had to come. I don't remember a thing that we did wrong without her telling a story for washing out the soul.

We saw the billowing smoke spurting upward from the large smoke stack and the huffing sound of the train engine chugging into the station. The huge black engine screeched to a stop, letting off steam with a loud spew from its side. We jumped back. The conductor set a step in front of the open door and began helping passengers off.

"Let's guess who the passengers are and where they're going," Shelly said.

A big man clambered from the step and lumbered over the wooden deck. His footsteps caused the aged boards to wheeze and groan like some monster with a bad case of asthma.

"I think he must be a cook," Bay said. "Cooks are always tasting of their food."

"He could be a rich plantation owner who has thousands of sharecroppers to do his work. That's why he's so fat. He doesn't get his exercise," I said.

A woman hurried past, pulling a little girl by her hand. The child was screaming for her lost penny. It had rolled through one of the openings between the planked deck. I wished I could be that little girl going to have some wonderful adventure. I certainly wouldn't be crying. Zeke pulled up on one of the deck's planks and Bay began squeezing under the platform.

"Y'all can't do that." Shelly pulled at Bay's legs. "Get out from under there or we'll go home."

"I see her penny. It's right here. Let me go." He squirmed loose.

"There are varmints under there. You'd better get back out right now." She put her hands on her hips.

"Okay, okay. I'm coming." Bay crawled out and showed us his penny. "I found it."

"You know who it belongs to. You've gotta give it back."

"But I crawled under that old porch to get it. That little girl never would do that."

Zeke leapt on the loose board like a spring grasshopper. It fell in place with a loud thud. A whoosh of dust settled.

"Stop it." Shelly jumped. "Are y'all trying to tear up this place?"

"I was fixing that loose board."

"You made it loose."

"It was already done. This old depot is falling apart. Somebody needs to fix it."

"Y'all leave it alone and go give that little girl her penny."

"What if it's not even the one she dropped. Huh? There could be hundreds of pennies under there. Lots of people drop money."

"Hey, let's get all the money out from under there," I said as I pulled at the board.

"Stop or we'll go home. I mean it," Shelly warned. "Y'all can't go around acting like a bunch of heathens."

"What if there's a fortune under there? We could be rich. Lots of folks do drop coins and they get lost through the cracks," I said. "We might even get enough money to ride the train."

Shelly thought for a minute. "I'm not crawling under there. I'll hold the board up for y'all. Only you gotta hurry up. There's people liable to walk this way."

We squeezed through the opening. It was drab and gloomy under the aged porch. It smelled worse than the old storm pit. I saw spider webs, but no money. I crawled back out disappointed and dusty.

"Did you find anything?"

"No. Nothing but spider webs." I brushed at my hair.

Zeke and Bay came out with only a few coins and our hearts sank. We wouldn't be rich, but we could stop at the store. Bay went to the little girl and handed her a penny.

"Here, I found your money."

"My penny!" she squealed.

"Tell the little boy 'thank you'." The woman patted Bay's head. "You are so sweet. Just the nicest little gentleman I've ever met." She commended him on his good deed and thoughtfulness. Bay blushed.

The engineer stood talking to Mr. Grey. He smiled. "How's the time going? I know you've been eyeballing that pocket watch of yours."

"Yep, but don't you go letting the cat out of the bag. The truth is I couldn't tell you where the hands are pointing on this thing. This old pocket watch belonged to my daddy. Rest his soul. I can hear it ticking and all I know is that I'm still around to hear it." He laughed and mashed the timepiece to his ear. "Ah, perfect ticking," he said as he walked into the station.

He tipped his hat to Mrs. Annie McBride. She stepped out with a birdcage and a flowered straw hat. Its ribbon ties were folding and unfolding in the soft breeze.

Suddenly, our dog Blackie, who had been tending to his own business, decided to leap upon Mrs. Annie to see what she was holding. This caused her to drop the cage. The lid busted open and the bird flew out. I saw the fluttering of tiny feathers screeching and darting about. The woman called and whistled after it.

Zeke grabbed hold of Blackie and scolded him. Mr. Grey took off to help Mrs. Annie. He ran while scooping at the air with his prized Panama hat. His son had brought it back from a trip to Mexico. We never saw that canary again. Mrs. Annie told us it was such a shame that the poor little thing would more than apt die in the wild.

"Y'all ought not to have brought that dog up here," she said.

"Yes Ma'am," Zeke apologized. "I'm sorry. He don't usually act like that. He's a pretty good ol' dog. He ain't never been around a caged up bird. We didn't know he would do that."

Mrs. Annie didn't say anything. She rolled her eyes and huffed.

The train left. We listened to its lonesome whistle echoing in the distance. I closed my eyes and pretended, for just a minute, that I was going with it. I was ashamed of myself for being envious of that little girl. She might have been an orphan. What if she had been riding those orphan trains all her life? Maybe this woman adopted her. Maybe this was going to be her first, real, great adventure. Maybe that penny was her lucky penny or maybe it was special because her birth date was on it. I hoped she was seeing things too wonderful to be believed. Maybe she was seeing a city with tall buildings.

I breathed a sigh and went on daydreaming. I dreamed of a beautiful land somewhere…a land where the fields were lovely, flowering meadows…a land with white lattice-laced gazebos resting in shady arbors of morning glory vines…a place where no one worked in the hot sun or went barefoot. Clothes weren't patched or worn out from working the dusty fields. They were white and smelled clean, like lilacs and roses.

"Hey, the train's gone. We gotta go home and finish chopping the weeds." Shelly's voice intruded.

"You must really like chopping weeds." I was upset about being interrupted from my thoughts. "You just can't wait to get back to it. Can you?"

"Well, stay here and daydream till the cows come home for all I care." She flounced her back to me and began walking home. The hem of her flour sack dress was pinched up in the back and her bony knees were showing.

"I'm coming," I said as I stepped off the platform and onto the dusty ground. "Here, you can have this." I handed her my lucky charm. It was real lucky because the magic had rubbed off on it from Mable Lee. She was a voo-doo woman who lived down at the last sharecropper's cabin. She knew all about magic, hexing, and conjuring up all sorts of stuff. She'd dip snuff and spit in a Mason's jar. One time she let me taste her snuff and it burned my mouth.

"What's this?" Shelly looked at the token.

"It's a good luck piece. I made it myself." I had put a string through its small, square hole so it could be worn around the neck like any other valuable amulet.

"You're supposed to wear it for good luck."

"How come I never saw this before?"

"I just made it. That's why."

"Then how do you know if its lucky or not?"

"Cause I know about magic and stuff like that. Mable Lee has the gift you know. I reckon that token might be even more powerful than a rabbit's foot, horse's shoe or even a four-leaf clover."

"Thanks." She pulled the string over her head.

I was glad she wasn't mad at me anymore for snapping at her. I hated it when my 'little fits of temper' got the better of me. Somehow Shelly could rile me so easily. Just like last week. We'd gone home for dinner and a rest from the fields. I had tried to ignore the work whistle. I wanted to pretend that I was asleep and hadn't heard it blowing.

She punched me and yelled, "Clair, it's time to go. The whistle has blown. Get up."

I'd hopped off the bed and yelled back at her. I told her that I'd rather be beaten a million times over than to work in that blistering hot sun. I said my fingers were sore from the sticking and my back was tired from bending over and dragging that sack. Besides all that, my feet were blistered from the hot dusty ground and I was sunburned. "You can't wait to get me back out there. Can you miss overseer? Just who are you to order us back to the fields to pick?"

She'd quietly said, "I know it's hard. I wish I could pick for us all. I hate that anyone has to work in the fields."

I felt so bad. I hated myself for being so hateful. I wanted to be strong, kind, gentle and everything I should be. I wished I could have eaten my words or crawled inside myself and disappeared all together.

Shelly did say that we could take the long way home. On our way, we passed the river bend where the fish would almost jump on the stringer. As Zeke said, "We gotta hide behind a tree to bait our hook."

It's the river that had the third trestle…the trestle that had the ghost train running and whistling over it when there was no train in sight. Its the ghost train James had told us about. Every one of us had, at one time or another, heard the ghost train. Some folks claimed to have seen it running over their lands, its headlight blazing a fiery trail through the night as it went whistling by. Others have said that on foggy nights you could see the brakeman walking along the tracks swinging his lantern back and forth while moaning. His haunting cries could be heard echoing through the trees. They say that on some nights he comes knocking at the doors and waking folks up.

The smell of ripe cotton swept though the musty air as we walked along. A mocking bird spread its white-laced wings and soared into the limbs of a gnarled oak tree. It lost itself in the ruffling and swaying of dense leaves. Shelly stopped and began to pick a bouquet of early blooming black-eyed Susans. Bay climbed on the fence while Zeke caught dragonflies. I wanted to pick the flowers too.

Shelly said I couldn't because she'd thought of it first. "And you needn't think you can add flowers to mine and take credit for the idea."

I bent down and started to pick some flowers of my own.

"You can't copy either," she said.

"You're just being mean." I wished that I'd thought of taking Mother a bouquet first. Shelly never missed thinking of good things to do. As we walked on she proudly arranged her bouquet. I felt jealous that she had such a pretty bunch. I knew Mother would love them. She'd give Shelly a big hug and kiss. Then she'd tell her how wonderful it was of her to gather them. I could see it already.

We came to the Granger's place. In the ditch was a whole spray of wildflowers. These were bigger and prettier than the ones Shelly had.

"Oh, Clair. I'll tell Mother you helped gather the bouquet if you'll crawl down there and pick those for me." She pointed at the ditch.

"But Mr. Granger is outside. He'll see me."

Folks say Mr. Granger is addlepated or shellshocked because of the war. In 1912 he and nearly four million Americans went with General Pershing to fight in the World War. Some German had shot and killed the Austrian heir to the throne. Then the whole world had gotten pulled into fighting. Most every time anyone passed Old Man Granger's place, he was outside walking in a wide circle. He called it his "thinking path". The path had worn down past his ankles and it was a fairly new one. We were shy of him.

"He won't even notice you. He's too busy walking and grumbling."

I thought of Mother and how happy she would be with the bouquet. I edged into the ditch and began pulling the wildflowers. I could see Mr. Granger with his head down and his arms folded behind his back. He walked that circle, mumbled, and raved. He was getting louder. He sounded like he was arguing with someone. He took his hat off and threw it hard against the ground.

"Dad gum sorry sight I say. Dad gum sorry sight." He reached down and scooped up the hat. Then he plopped it back on his head. He stretched his neck toward me. I quickly crawled back upon the road. His teeth were crooked and gaped with wide spaces. They looked like a fence that had been left unattended, weathered and falling.

I held the flowers up. "I didn't think you'd mind."

He pulled at the sides of his floppy hat. I noticed that his faded, blue overalls were missing a button. They were flapping open on one side.

"Can't you see? Just lookie here." He snatched the overalls open. "My whole tail end is nearly hanging out and what's she doing? She's hunting for a safety pin. Who'd ever thought that she wouldn't take the time to sew on a button? Dang sorry sight…me standing here near buck and she's hunting a pin."

"Yes, Sir." We hurried down the road.

He went back to his "thinking path" and continued grumbling, "I'm gonna pin up my drawers but when I go to bend over that pin's more than apt gonna pop and stab out my blasted appendix. Reckon she'll be happy when that happens. Reckon she will."

As we hurried down the road Bay started giggling. He tried to hold back his laughter by mashing his hand across his mouth. He made loud whistling and snorting sounds.

"Shush." Shelly pulled him by his free hand. "You're not supposed to laugh at him."

"But did you see his *toomie*?" He busted out laughing.

Suddenly, we all laughed and ran. Our word for the naked behind was *toomie*.

I handed Shelly the flowers I'd picked. She arranged them with her bouquet. We passed the tall growing broom sage fields where the sawmill sat. In the evenings, when no one was there, it loomed before us like a scene from some forgotten ghost town. The lumber stacks and sawdust piles waited against the dusky skyline. The windows and doors were empty, gaping black holes. The evening wind sang through them while the night owls hooted from the rafters.

When we got home the sun was sinking below the horizon. It turned the skyline into a fiery display of vivid colors. We finished chopping the last few bitter weeds and took our hoes to the shed as the earth absorbed the last few bars of twilight. The lengthening shadows oozed like slow-moving molasses to cover the world in darkness.

We went inside. I thought about what Grandma always said. "You gotta work from kin to kan't. From when you kin see till when when you kan't see." And she'd laugh.

Inside the cabin the lamplight flickered over the walls. It cast frolicking shadows on the old gray boards. Something from the oven smelled good. Daddy sat at the table rosining up his bow. The bow's many strings split if they weren't well coated with the rosin. The fiddle had been his Grandpa's. Its rich brown wood glistened like new.

I watched Daddy poke the handsome instrument under his neck. He rested his chin in its black chin cup. When he swept the newly rosined bow over the strings it sent our hearts to dancing and his foot to tapping.

Zeke whispered in my ear. "You know what you smell cooking don't you? It's a possum. Daddy went hunting and bagged it. Don't you know that opossum is nothing more than a woods rat?"

"Well, Mother wouldn't cook it if it wasn't good to eat," I said.

"Clair, bring the lamp over here a minute. I think this rascal is about ready."

I shuddered when she called it a "rascal". I thought about what Zeke had told me. I didn't want to eat a rat. I put the freshly cleaned globe over the lighted wick and walked to the stove.

Mother bent over and pulled the large pan out of the oven. It smelled and looked like a big, juicy roast. Sweet potatoes circled the meat, gravy bubbled all around. She placed it in the center of the table. I put the lamp behind it and couldn't help noticing how delicious it looked. Mother added a bowl of peas, platter of cornbread, some sassafras tea and milk to the table.

I pumped water into the face pan and washed my hands and face. The pan was milk white enamel, trimmed around its edge with a bright red rim. Anyone caught using the face pan for anything but face and hands was scolded in the worst way. There was a foot pan for the feet and other parts of the body. Every night we had to wash our feet in the foot pan before going to bed.

On Saturday night a big washtub was used for an all over bath. In wintertime it was put in the kitchen and water was pumped and heated on the stove. In summer the tubs of sun-warmed water were carried into the smokehouse. If the water had to be drawn from the well it was put in the sun to warm.

Zeke and Bay combed their hair and put on clean shirts before sitting at the table. Men and boys must never come to the table without being well-groomed. Bay's hair was shinning with Vitalis hair tonic. "Look how nice Bay looks, Daddy." Mother said. "Ever since he got that whipping for coming to breakfast without combing his hair, there's never been a neater boy. In fact, the first thing that child does when he wakes up is comb his hair."

"What beats all is him standing there combing his hair with a cyclone bearing down on us." Daddy said. Mother laughed while remembering that stormy night. Daddy had run through the house waking everyone to go to the storm pit. We all ran but Bay. He was standing in front of the mirror combing his hair.

"You sure did teach that one a lesson. He might forget a lot of things, but he won't forget to comb his hair again, I grant you."

Shelly surprised Mother with the bouquet of wildflowers. We had found a shiny brown crock in the shed. The orange and deep brown of the flowers were a perfectly matched set of colors for the crock.

"Oh, how pretty." Mother threw her hands up in surprise. "I have always adored black-eyed Susans. Don't they look elegant decorating the supper table? Thank you, girls." She hugged and kissed us. "Supper will taste so much better with these sitting on the table."

Daddy said grace and ushered in the meal by lifting a forkful of food to his mouth.

At bedtime I told Mother about our rooster's funeral. I told her how Shelly had stood on the tree root, like we all did when we had some performance to give, and how she'd read from the Holy Bible.

"That's the hardest kind of reading there is, isn't it?"

"Some say so. Mighty hard unless you know the author real well."

We snuggled down in bed as the whippoorwills called to the night crickets. I asked Shelly if she reckoned I might ever read such writings some day.

"When you get in third grade you can if you want to."

She was in the third grade.

"I want to."

Chapter Four

Trouble with Fly Bread and Moonshine

THE sun was already hot on my back at only eight in the morning. I trudged along pulling the cotton from each sharp bole and shoved it into my sack. I talked to Zeke on the other side of the row. We were having one of our races to see who could pick the fastest and the most.

"I wish I had a way to hook forks on a wagon wheel. I'd roll it through the field so that it could pull the cotton out for me. All I'd have to do then is stuff it in my sack," he said.

"You're just full of ideas, Zeke. Good ones too. It would probably work if you could find the stuff to make it with." I thought about the guitar he'd made from rubber bands. He had stretched four tightly over a matchbox. It could really make music. "You're going to be an inventor when you grow up."

"You think so, Clair?"

"Yeah. Mrs. Neal says that you ain't nothing but a hyperactive idea factory all wrapped up in skin. You just running around like an ant on a bed of hot rocks seeing what you can conjure up next."

Sadie May in the next row pulled past us. Her three-month-old twins were curled up on top of her cotton sack that she drug behind her. She had just come in from nursing them under the big sweet gum tree at the edge of the field.

"Hi Sadie!"

"Howdy do! Y'all sure are getting along with your picking today looks like. What's done set a fire under you young'uns?"

"We're racing to the end of the row and trying to catch up with Maxine."

"Oh, I see." The little babies rested on the fluffy cotton in the shade of the cotton stalks. I looked down on them as she pulled ahead of us.

Suddenly, many panic-driven screams echoed around us. We looked up to see what all the commotion was about. A rabid dog had come into the field. He was growling and foam dribbled from his snarling mouth. Sadie screeched and grabbed her babies with cotton sack and all. She took off like a wild woman. Her long legs hopped through the cotton stalks like a stampeding gazelle. Everybody lit into running and screaming. Shelly grabbed Bay's hand and raked him through the stalks like a sack. She pulled him toward Mother who was frantically running toward us.

She got behind us yelling, "Get to the scale wagon! Get to the scale wagon!"

As we ran through the field we laid the cotton stalks low. It looked like some sudden strong wind had swept through and nearly cleared the land. In the stampede clothes, legs and bodies were ripped to shreds and bloodied from the sharp cotton boles. A frantic wave of people washed over the field toward Mr. Harris and the scale wagon.

Mr. Harris, the tally man, had been resting in the wagon's shade when he heard the commotion. He looked up and saw the pickers running toward him. He heard them screaming. "Rabid Dog! Rabid dog!"

He grabbed his shotgun and took off toward the crazed animal. It was stalking and growling through the empty field. A loud shot echoed through the countryside, then another and it was all over. The mad dog lay dead in the field. Just as quiet settled and everyone breathed a sigh of relief, Sadie May's shrill yell rang out. "I lost one of my babies! The mad dog ate my baby!"

She groped through the bundle.

James grabbed her and said, "Is this what you're looking for?"

"My baby!" She squealed as he opened the bib of his overalls and there, curled up on his chest, was the infant girl.

"If I hadn't been behind you, the baby would have been trampled to death," he said. "I saw her when she slipped out of the sack. It's a thousand wonders she wasn't killed."

"A thousand wonders we weren't all killed." Sadie rested against him. She held her babies and thanked James for being there to save little

May. "I just knew that snarling mad dog had got her."

Daddy looked at Mother and said, "Just look at your legs. It looks like you lost a cat fight."

"No, I won a race with a mad dog. Let me tell you one thing. I could have sworn I felt his breath on my heels a few times. Now I know why men wear pants. I don't see scrapes on you." She laughed.

"My scrapes are in my mind. This has ripped my nerves to shreds. I thought several times y'all were going to be trampled to death. That scared me worse than the dog."

Mr. Harris told two men to go and get rid of the animal.

"Be sure not to touch it. The rest of you can call it a day."

"That's a good idea. I don't want the kids back out in that field where that rabid dog drool is anyway," Mother said.

Mable Lee, the voodoo woman, came huffing by as we were walking away. "You can't give a dog fly bread. It'll go flat out mad. Somebody done give that dog fly bread."

Floyd came up behind us with his face as red as a boiled beet.

"I really don't know what you gots to be afraid of, Floyd. One smell of you would run any ol' dog off, mad or not." Maxine laughed as she ran toward me. "Ain't that right, Clair."

"Sure is." I smiled at her. "Floyd probably gave that dog the rabies." We both laughed. Floyd tore off running toward us with a look that said, 'I'm gonna beat the tar out of y'all.' I ran faster to catch up with Mother as Maxine fled toward Boo.

We walked on toward the cabin. Zeke asked, "What kind of bread is fly bread? I heard Mable Lee say that's the kind of bread that makes mad dogs."

"Oh, Zeke. That's just her way of saying flour bread."

"Why does she say it different?" I asked.

"Everyone says stuff in their own way Clair. Sometimes the way you say things may sound strange to people who don't talk like you."

"That makes sense Mother."

We were satisfied. We skipped ahead to catch up with Shelly and

Bay. No matter how we got this free day I was going to enjoy it. I could rest and play the day away.

Daddy decided to load some sugar cane and take it to the mill to be made into syrup. We would get a ripe stalk to chew. We followed him to the barn as he carried the stalks out and stacked them on the wagon bed. I saw a couple of field mice scamper for the hills. "We didn't get to this any too soon," Daddy said as he scooped up another armload.

We picked out a nice long stalk that had turned purple. These were the sweetest ones. We'd cut the stalk into pieces and peel its hard sides back and chew the soft pulpy insides. Its sweet juice tasted better than a candy bar.

"While I'm gone Zeke, you and Clair clean out the cow pen."

"Yes, sir," we said as we laid our sugar cane on the porch. It could wait until we were done with our chore. There never was an end to working around here. Seems like to me that Daddy invented stuff for us to do. We moved the cow piles to the edge of the trees. We had a bucket with a stick put through the handle. Zeke held one side while I held the other as we carried it off. When we got back there was one pile that we had missed, so we decided to cover it with dirt so Daddy couldn't see it. Then we sat down to chew our sugar cane.

Zeke had found a forked limb at the edge of the trees, "This will make a great slingshot if I can find an old inner tube. I have a shoe tongue for the pocket."

"Mr. Roberts has some old car parts in the barn. He may have some inner tubes too. But what are you going to shoot with it?"

"Well, if any more wild dogs come around we'll need protection. We can practice shooting at cans with it."

We walked across the pasture to Mr. Roberts' barn. Inside Zeke found a nice inner tube. He cut two strips from it with his rusty pocketknife. He tied the strips of rubber onto his forked stick. Then he jabbed two holes in the shoe tongue and hooked it onto the strips. He took a pebble and tried it out. The pebble flew clear to the back of the barn and hit the wall with a loud thud.

"That's the best one I've ever made," he said as he stuck it in the bib pocket of his overalls.

On our way home, he poked a wooden sword at an invisible foe while he took swipes at his unruly hair. It liked to rest on his forehead despite him training it with hair tonic.

Suddenly he yelled, "Dang a mile, run!"

He took off. His shirttail flapped behind him. It looked like wings. I thought he could fly to the top of one of the hickory nut trees with a little more speed. I looked behind me and saw Mr. Roberts' prize bull. It was charging straight at us. I struck out like a panther cat on Zeke's heels. My feet got tangled in a clump of weeds and I sailed onto the ground. I splatted against it like a skillet-flipped fritter cake. I laid there groaning for air while Zeke rolled under the fence and stood yelling for me to run.

Run? I couldn't even crawl. I wondered if he didn't suppose that I'd be in the next county by now if my feet could have kept up with my mind. Zeke thought I was hurt and crawled back through the fence to help me. He began slapping and scrapping at the air, while yelling at the bull. The wild-eyed animal snorted, pawed the ground and walled its ugly eyes at us. I jumped up, running until we were safe under the fence.

"You were running faster than the sheriff's bloodhounds." I told Zeke.

"I noticed you kicked up a little dust yourself," he said.

We walked through the tall corn stalks. The leaves patted against us like long green arms. It was as if they were congratulating us on our narrow escape. A soft wind made them rustle and whisper over the field.

"Zeke you are the bravest person I know. You were going to fight that charging bull."

"I wasn't brave. I was really afraid."

"Well, I think that must be what it means to be brave, you know… doing something that you are afraid to do."

"You may be right. But I don't feel very brave."

"But you are. Who else would have jumped in front of a mad bull?"

We took the long way home around Mr. Robert's pasture to avoid his bull. On our way we passed Mrs. Neal's place. She was sitting on her front porch swing laughing and talking with Brother Paul.

"You see that?" I said. "I saw them down in the woods having a picnic. I thought that they had accidentally run into each other. It must have been planned. They're awful sweet on each other. Don't you think?"

"She'd better watch out or Mrs. Effie will run her out of town on a rail."

"Yep, after she tars and feathers her."

"Did you know about Mrs. Effie and Mr. Grey down at the store kissing on each other?"

"Well, don't that beat all. Mrs. Effie's being like an old sitting hen, just cackling to throw suspicion off herself. If a hen cackles you don't have to go look, you know there's an egg in the nest." As we came towards our tree house we noticed the rope ladder swinging. "Something's in the tree house," I whispered as I put my hand out to stop Zeke. "Look at the ladder swinging."

"Yeah, I see it," he whispered back. "Gotta be something big to make a rope swing like that."

"Get your slingshot out so you can shoot it. I'll scare it out." I picked up a handful of pebbles and rocks and came up behind the tree house yelling at the top of my lungs and bombed the house with the rocks. Two big fat bobcats dropped to the ground and bounded off toward the woods.

Zeke was frozen still.

"You didn't even shoot at them! What if that had been rabid dogs in there? Would you have just stood there and let them tear you limb from limb?"

"I need to learn how to shoot at moving targets I guess. Until I do let's be sure to keep up all the fly bread." We laughed as we walked home.

We noticed Daddy out in the cow pen inspecting it. He was walking very near the spot where we'd hidden the cow pile. "Oh, Zeke! I hope he doesn't see what we did." About that time Daddy's foot landed right in the covered pile.

"Dad gum it!" He hollered out. "Zeke, Clair! Come over here!" We both started pleading our case at the same time.

"But Daddy, there was only one more. We didn't want to walk all that way with just one."

"If I've taught you kids one thing, its to do your job the best you can. Now, is this the best you could have done?"

"No sir. I'm sorry," We both said as we hung our heads.

"Then y'all will finish this job right and clean my boots, won't you?"

"Yes, sir."

It was nearing supper that evening that Sheriff Springer came to our cabin with a passel of other men-folk from around town. Jack and Dude Hicks, from outlaw hollow, had robbed Mr. Grey's store and the sheriff was gathering up a posse. "I'll get my gun." Daddy said as he rushed back into the cabin.

"Be careful, Cooper." Mother said as she kissed him.

"I'll be back in a minute, keep the supper hot." He took the boot I was cleaning patted me on the head, "good job, Clair." He smiled at me as he shoved his foot down in it and rushed out the door.

Now, Jack and Dude were two of the most ornery fellows around. They lived down there in the hollows where outlaws gathered. They seldom came around town except to gather or steal supplies. It had been known as 'outlaw hollow' since right after the Civil War. The one old man who started it was meaner then the devil himself. He'd shoot his own young'un to get a chaw of tobacco. He'd just soon shoot you as look at you. He was that mean. They say he killed his little girl and his wife. The child had spilled water on him and he slapped her stone cold dead right then and there.

When his wife came at him he choked the life out of her. He buried them both in a shallow grave in his backyard. His son cowered in a corner and watched until he could get away. Then the boy told the authorities everything. When they came out after the old man he ran down into these hollows.

During the Civil War he encouraged deserters from both sides to join him and stockpile army supplies in his hideout. They'd even rob dead men on the battlefield to get anything of value, even taking their shoes and clothes and leaving the poor fellows naked as a jaybird. They didn't care what they had to do to get supplies. They were vicious and ungodly. They had no ethics, no morals, no love and no concern for anything holy or unholy.

Their sole ambition was to get all they could any way they could get it. They only ventured out in the dark of night to go pilfering and gathering their ill-gotten gains. They stole pigs, cows, chickens and whatever they wanted from the local farmers. They festered down in those wild, woodsy hollows like a plague waiting to spread its ugliness. Their band had grown from here all the way over to Sullivan Hollow in Lamar County. Vast logging and strict law was thinning them out, leaving only the most harmless ones, while trying to instill civility and education in them.

Jack and Dude's mother, Martha Hicks, was an old widow woman about as mean as, if not meaner, than they. She used to haul lighter knots to town. Everyone knew that they had them a big old still down yonder in the hollows.

Tonight Jack and Dude had broken into Mr. Grey's store and stole a whole load of corn mash, sugar and stuff. The sheriff had grabbed his gun, old Gunther and Tate, his twin bloodhounds, and some of the other men folk to go down in the hollows after them.

Later Daddy would tell us about when they got to the house. He said Sheriff Springer knocked on the porch and yelled for Jack and Dude to come on out of the house.

Mrs. Hicks came out on the porch. She was madder than a wet hen and toting a double barrel shotgun. She yelled, "Get on away from here a fore I shoot your tails off!"

The two boys had come out and stood beside her with mud up to their knees. They held their lamps high, as they tried to see. Dude had asked, "Hey Sheriff, is that you?"

"Yeah, Dude. It me," Sheriff Springer had said. "Have you boys been down to Mr. Grey's store this here evening?"

"They ain't been nowhere!" Martha Hicks yelled as she spat a wad of snuff on the ground at the sheriff's feet. She pointed the gun at him but the sheriff had just kept on talking.

"Move that thing out of my face Martha before you dislodge them rusty shells." He pushed the gun barrel away from his face. "Why don't you boys round up that stuff you took and come on along to jail," he'd said. "It's gonna get hotter than a billy goat in a pepper patch around here if y'all don't."

Then old lady Hicks had commenced yelling. "Sheriff you can't expect my boys to give back all that stuff and go off to jail too!" She explained that if they gave back the stuff then they hadn't ought to go to jail for stealing. In the end though, they did follow the sheriff to the jailhouse to work off every penny they owed. Mrs. Hicks did keep the stuff and is down there making moonshine like crazy.

Old lady Hicks had about twenty kids down in that hollow. They ran around snot-nosed, barefooted and ragged. They never went to school or church, in fact, they hardly ever went anywhere.

One day, back in early summer, Jack, Dude and Martha Hicks loaded them up on the back of the flatbed truck and tore off into town. Once or twice a year they got to go into town to get a piece of candy from Mr. Grey's store. While speeding down the country road Jack hit a bump. One flew off and landed in the ditch…the ditch where we gathered crawdads for fishing bait. They didn't miss her till they got to town. That's when one of the young'uns said, "Since Inez fell off the truck and is dead now, can I have her share of the candy?"

"Where she fall off at?" Mrs. Hicks asked.

They reluctantly told her. Jack ran out of the store to pick her up. Martha Hicks looked over at Mr. Grey with a puzzled expression. She said, just as serious as could be, "I been wondering what's been goin' with them young'uns. I thought maybe there was an alligator on the loose."

Little Inez Hicks had only a few scrapes and bruises. Nothing she wasn't used to.

Ever so often old lady Hicks would come out of the hollow with another snot-nosed young'un on her hip. We all wondered where they were coming from while she wondered where they'd been going.

Chapter Five

Big Fish and Folks

THE early morning duskiness hid the horizon and owls still hooted from the shadowed trees when Mother and Daddy left. I watched them go to begin their day in the field. Strong, committed, determined and quietly talking together, their soft voices in reverence for the newborn day. The cotton fields were about picked clean now and we had a few more days before school would start again. We had this time to do whatever we wanted.

There was a lonesome atmosphere in the drab cabin without Mother's cheerful face. She made our lives happy and complete. I wiped the dewiness from the windowpane. I watched as Mr. Harris passed leading the mules to the barn. His head was down and slowly bobbing in time with his steps. I wondered if he knew he was being watched.

The Harris' live in the cabin across the road from Mable Lee's. They have lived there longer than anybody and their cabin looks like a regular house. It has been whitewashed with a room and large porch added on. All around their house is a white fence with red rose vines growing up it. Over the years they have woven in and out along the entire length of the fence. When the deep red roses are in full bloom the sweet smell fills the air around the Harris' place.

I hoped that someday our cabin would look like that. In our desire to have a place like this, me and Zeke found a bottle of white shoe polish and started to paint our cabin. But we ran out before we got a decent square done. I thought a whole bottle would have done all of our cabin and Zeke thought so too. What a disappointment that had been!

Mr. Harris is the one who weighs in the bags of cotton, writes the tally in the books and empties the cotton into the wagon. He picks on the little kids by pretending to strain really hard to pick up their cotton sacks. Even when their tiny lumps don't weigh-in he gives them a penny anyway. Everyone likes the tallyman. We all idolize him for saving us from that mad dog. All of us think he is a hero.

Mr. Taylor, the iceman, stopped in front of the cabin. He began lugging a heavy block of ice on tongs to the icebox. He chipped it to fit then patted me on the head and left.

Zeke got up and said, "Let's go fishing. I'll dig the worms and I'll bait your hook, Shelly. I'll even take the fish off the hook for you." We all knew Shelly hated to touch worms or fish, even though she liked catching them right enough.

"No thanks," Shelly said. She walked outside with her embroidery basket. "I want to work on my mantle scarf." She sat on a bench under the gnarled chinaberry tree and began threading her needle. Bay sat in the dirt with his lead soldiers making forts and rock castles for his troops to defend.

"I'm gonna stay here with Shelly," he said. "I don't like smelly ol' fish either."

Bay liked fishing when he caught a fish. Most times he would get upset if his cork didn't bob the second he dropped the hook in the water. He was still too young to understand the art of fishing.

Zeke and I took our poles from under the porch, then marched off toward the woods where the river cut through the trees. As we crossed through a barbed wire fence, I caught my hair on one of the coils. I tried to untangle it, but a few strands of knotted hair dangled on the barb as I crawled through. I rubbed my scalp and looked around.

A hawk flew overhead in a wide circle then back to the far hills satisfied that we weren't animals that needed his attention. The woods came alive with the chattering of birds and squirrels. They seemed to have a signal among themselves that buzzed to the ends of the forest. It said, "People are in the woods. Better be careful and watch out!"

Tall reeds, the kind we used for making our fishing poles, grew thickly along the creek bank. The stream wound its way through the tall trees and flowed over the beaver's dam like a rushing waterfall. We carefully started walking to get to the other side of the bank. About the time we got part way out the sound of the ghost train echoed through the woods. It sounded so close that we sat on the dam and waited for the thing to take us to kingdom come.

We knew it had come for us. We closed our eyes and held onto each other while the rushing water swished around us. Some folks say that the ghost train comes around to pick up passengers and take them to the hereafter. Neither of us wanted to go on to Glory right then, so we sat there, clasping each other and yelling. We yelled until the sound was long gone.

Zeke and I looked at each other to see if we were still here. His big blue eyes were as round as saucers and I suppose mine were too. "I thought it had us for sure. Clair, do you think that was the real ghost train?"

"If there is one I think that must have been it."

The creek grew wider as it curved through the trees. Tall trees with their giant roots poking out of the banks like long wrinkled arms reached into the singing water. Mother would sometimes come fishing here for a few hours just to relax and watch the water flowing. She'd bring home a few tiny perch on a forked stick and fix them for supper. Daddy called them, "little wads of greasy bones" and told her that those fish weren't even weaned. He'd laughed. "The Mother of those little baby 'fishies' might hunt you down for keeping them."

We walked farther into the woods. There were gullies, ditches and bogs that we'd swing over on musky dine vines. I thought the long swing was like flying. I dropped to the other side and threw the vine back to Zeke. The dry, rotted leaves made a thick carpet through the woods and the sunlight dancing through the trees made patterns on them. We saw places where the leaves were turned. They were darker and wetter; probably an Armadillo had been rooting around looking for food. We saw a stump with rabbit droppings scattered on top. "I wonder if mother rabbits make children rabbits go to this stump like we go to the outhouse?" Zeke asked.

"I think they must. Remember what Granny told us about how smart rabbits are?"

Granny was most always expecting something wonderful from each new day. She'd rise early to milk the cows singing as she went. One cold Easter morning, she took her milk pails and started walking through the pasture to the barn. She spied a whole passel of bunnies in a circle standing on their back legs and playing "Patty Cake" together. No one could persuade her that she hadn't been a witness to Easter bunnies at play. Every Easter she told that same story.

"Yeah, I remember, and I do think that stump must be their toilet."

We came upon a quiet little cove where the dark water seemed to be resting against the sloping banks. We sat under a tall sycamore with its golden umbrella-sized leaves swaying overhead. They rustled on the warm autumn breeze. I watched the patterns of shade on the forest floor as they jumped and moved about. Our corks bobbed and rocked on the murky water.

Tiny doodlebug holes were scattered over the ground. A doodlebug is a scary looking creature, white and wiggly with that big brown head. It looks like a lion's mane on top of its fat wormy body. We loved catching these doodlebugs. It was pretty easy because they're very tidy creatures. If anything gets in their house or blocks their doorway they won't rest till they get it out. I broke off a long weed stem and poked it down into a doodlebug's tunnel. It was so deep that it nearly swallowed the whole stem. The invading stem culprit rested there only a few seconds before the bug grabbed a hold of it. I could tell by the trembling of the weed that the thing had taken hold. When the doodlebug had worked the stem nearly all the way up I snatched it out faster than lightning. The bug was caught! He would do for bait so I added him to the can.

I wiped an ant off my foot then propped my chin on my drawn-up knee. A ladybug crawled up a blade of grass. I put out my finger and she crept upon it and tickled my finger as she crawled toward my hand. I whispered, "Ladybug, Ladybug, fly away home," and watched as her delicate wings unfolded and swept her into the air. A spider worked over a sticky web. A field mouse scurried through a clump of thistles and dried leaves.

Suddenly Zeke began yelling at the top of his lungs.

"I've got one! I've got one! It's a big one." He yanked his line up so hard that he slung that fish, hook, line and sinker up into the tall sycamore. It caught solid in the thick branches and hung there. "It's a whopper!" He was screaming and running to go up the tree after the dangling fish.

As he shinnied up the tree the fish's flopping paid off and it came sailing down. It hit the ground with a plopping thud as Zeke screamed, "Don't let him get away!" In the excitement I threw myself over the tumbling fish.

Suddenly I realized what I'd done and commenced yelling frantically in fear for my life. "It's gonna bite my stomach! It's gonna fin me! Hurry. Hurry and get it!" I kept screaming. "I feel its fins! Help!"

Zeke reached for the fish as I rolled off it. As he grasped it in both hands, the slimy thing gave a sudden twist and went cascading down the slippery bank into the dark water. I believe I saw a tear in Zeke's eye. He said, "That's the biggest fish I've ever caught in my entire life."

"Well, it's down there swimming around with a giant hare lip now. You yanked half its mouth off when you jerked it out of the water. I'll bet he's down there telling all the other fish about his narrow escape."

"Yeah, if they can understand a hare-lipped fish." Zeke laughed "It was a whopper though wasn't it Clair?"

"The biggest ever," I said.

We picked up our poles and started home. We came to the old creek bridge. Mrs. Neal was standing at the water's edge gathering the pretty rocks and putting them in her basket. She smiled and waved.

"Y'all have any luck?" she asked.

"We caught one, but it got away," I said.

"A big one." Zeke threw his hands out in measurement.

"Well, now. Don't you know that it's always the big ones that get away?" She turned and twisted a rock in her fingers before adding it to her basket.

"We do now." Zeke said as we walked on.

Mrs. Neal, our teacher, was a widow woman. She liked to come to the creek and gather the different colored river rocks and pebbles. She made all kinds of pretty things and set them in her windows. She sometimes sold them.

I remember when Mother bought one of her rock creations and showed it to Daddy. He began to rant at her. "Madge, that's about as useless as teats on a boar hog. Why in sam hill would she pay good money for a blasted rock when they're laying all over the road? Give me the money and I'll go out there and pick up a whole handful for you."

But Mother said, "That's not the same thing and you know it. Look here. There's an honest to goodness cow's face on this rock."

Then Daddy had said, "It looks like a blasted old rock to me."

"Well, it's not. There's a cow's face on it. In fact, it looks a lot like ol' brownie's face."

But Daddy had said, "I've got better things to do than sit here all day trying to find a stupid thing like a cow's face on a plain simple rock."

That was the first and last rock that Mother ever bought. Yet there, on the shelf beside Great Great Grandma Jennie O'Brian's cream picture, sits Mrs. Neal's cow rock.

"I'll see you kids Monday." Mrs. Neal said as we walked on.

Mr. Ed and Mrs. Effie Clay came walking toward us. "Good evening." They spoke as they walked on over the sweet gum bayou bridge.

We cut through the woods toward home.

All of a sudden there was a racket of yelling and fussing down at the bridge. We were too far away to hear exactly what was being said, but we knew it wasn't good. We rushed back to the road as Mrs. Effie rushed past us clutching a hold of Mr. Clay's arm. We heard Mrs. Effie say, "Brother Paul is going to hear about this!"

Not far behind them was Mrs. Neal. "The very idea of that woman! She's as crazy as a loon!"

Zeke looked at me, "I wonder what that was all about?"

"I don't know, but with Mrs. Effie in it, you know its not good."

As we continued on our way, Joe Blass came stumbling toward us heading for a log that lay across the creek.

"A good day to you." He slurred his words. We could smell the strong liquor on his breath as he sat into philosophizing. He could lay out a good enough speech if he could find ears to listen. We were in a hurry and told him so as we trotted onward. He waved his arms in the air and told the trees that the world was just not ready for a mind like his. He stumbled toward the log as we looked back to see if he would fall.

"I don't think he's gonna make it this time," I said.

"Aw he'll make it. He's been walking logs like that all his life."

We watched him totter over the log and off toward that still of his.

"I guess he needs another sample of that mess."

Joe Blass usually sat around town drunk as a spun skunk, wearing a pair of dark glasses and singing those 'tearjerkers' and 'sinners beware' gospel songs. He waited for folks to drop money in his begging cup. Most everyone knew that Joe wasn't really blind, but they'd drop coins in his cup out of pity, I suppose. Or they knew that he needed supplies for his moonshine making still he thought he had hidden in the hollow. But everyone, except the revenuers knew where it was. The revenuers would come and destroy any still if they found out about it.

Joe Blass was one of our 'respectable' moonshiners. Sheriff Springer didn't care how many folks moonshined and neither did the towns-people. Just as long as the moonshiners got their supplies the right and legal way no one told the revenuers anything. Too many folks liked a little nip every now and then and white lightning was cheap. This part of the country produced more alcoholics than dogs have fleas.

"I wonder why Joe is always drunk? I know lots of people who have their fair share of spirits, but they're sober at least some of the time. But I've never seen him sober."

"I don't know. Maybe something happened to him." I said.

We walked on.

The fields of yellow-orange broom sage rippled in the breeze. Black-eyed Susans and golden rod mingled with the reds, browns and greens of autumn. The big hawk circled overhead.

When we got home Mother was poking and jabbing in the big, black wash pot, smoke from the fire was carried off by the breeze. She had come home early from the fields to wash the clothes.

"Oh good. You're back in time to help. Look at my white sheets. Every bird in the whole county has flown over and left droppings on them and just as soon as hung them out too. There must be something about white sheets hanging on the line that tempts birds."

I wondered if maybe a white sheet flapping in the wind could scare the mess out of them, like a ghost or something.

"We have to get the washing done for school. Bay certainly is going to miss having y'all around all day. It'll be so lonesome around here for a while."

As Mother and I hung the clothes I looked into her face, it was tired and sweaty from the day of hard work. She went back to poke in the pot as she wiped the sweat from her forehead. She took the long pole, brought out more steaming clothes and dropped them in the washtub. The clean smell of lye soap filled the air. Shelly came out while Mother was rinsing them.

"The peas are done. The cornbread is brown and ready to take out of the oven. Can I do it, Mother?"

"No. The skillet's almost too heavy for me. I'll do it, but you can come here and finish rinsing the clothes." The rest of the morning we spent working and getting ready for school.

It was later that evening when I saw Brother Paul pass by in his old T-model ford. He had Ed and Effie Clay with him and they were driving out towards Mrs. Neal's place. I hurried to find Zeke, Shelly and Bay.

"I just saw Brother Paul pass with the Clays! They're going out to Mrs. Neal's."

"Lets go see what's going on." Zeke said.

We ran out there and hid ourselves behind a row of thick hedge so we could hear everything that went on.

Mrs. Effie called the widow woman outside.

"What's bothering you now, Mrs. Clay?"

"You know exactly what's bothering me! You have, more than once caused my husband to lust and I've brought Brother Paul out here to speak to you before you cause Ed to commit adultery by lusting again."

"And how on earth have I done that, pray tell?"

"You know how! Today you had you skirt tails hoisted above your knees in plain sight of everyone! You can't be tempting men folk like that. It's women like you who get men in trouble. You must admit your sin and ask forgiveness."

Mrs. Neal looked fit to be tied as Mrs. Effie went on. "We are here to pray for you and your desires toward my husband."

The teacher's mouth dropped open. She stiffened her back. "Pray for me? Pray for me? Whatever for?" she said. "Are you rambling just to hear your own head rattle?"

Mrs. Effie was vexed. "You have been after Mr. Clay and you have shown your legs to him down yonder at the bridge. You caused him to lust. You know you did it on purpose. That's sinful!" Mrs. Effie yelled. "And not only that you fling yourself at Brother Paul every chance you get! Its time he sees what you really are, you brazen sinner!"

"Now I know for sure. You are a pure lunatic! Get out of my yard before I do sin all upside your head." Mrs. Neal looked over at Brother Paul. "Are you really here with this stupid heifer?"

He answered, "Well, I don't know what to say. I did want to hear what you had to say about her accusations though."

Mrs. Neal was flaming as she said, "Oh, I've got something to say alright and you better get out of here before I say it."

All the while Mrs. Effie was hollering, "You must ask forgiveness! You must atone for your sin. Repent, I say! Repent! Admit what you did!"

She kept yelling until Mrs. Neal climbed on a sawed off stump and jerked her dress tails up high. She stuck her behind out and twisted it from side to side right in their faces while yelling, "Lust all the way to hell you old crow!"

Mrs. Effie screamed, grabbed Mr. Clay by his arm and ran off down the road dragging him behind her. He pulled back in his struggle to continue gazing upon Mrs. Neal's unmentionables. Brother Paul looked fit to be tied. Mrs. Neal hopped down off the stump and went stomping toward the house.

"My goodness gracious me Mrs. Neal," he said as he wiped at his forehead.

"Don't you go goodnessing me." Mrs. Neal whirled around. "I'm the one to say such."

She sailed into the house and slammed the door behind her.

All four of us were giggling and laughing out loud. "Mrs. Neal showed her toomie!"

We looked around as Brother Paul let out a deep cough. He had come over to where we were laughing and stood glaring at us. "Is this all so funny to you?" He folded his arms across his chest. His face was as red as a boiled beet. "Well, I hope you'll take a lesson from this and always remember to mind your own business. Maybe you'll stay out of trouble that way. Now, if Mrs. Neal needs prayer, or feels like she's sinned, she knows where the churches are." He squared his shoulders and walked away as he said, "Y'all get on home now. The show's over."

We stopped laughing. "Yes sir." We said as we hurried away.

On our way home Zeke looked at me. "Clair, have you ever lusted?"

"I don't know what lusting is, but its a sin. Mrs. Effie said so."

"Well what on earth is it about a girl legs that could cause anyone to lust and sin?"

"I guess it's only a woman's legs that causes lust. If our legs would cause lust then we'd all be guilty of lusting, I reckon, because we've seen an awful lot of legs."

Bay held up one leg, then the other as he sang out, "Lust left lust right. Lust left, lust right."

"I don't think that's what that means," Shelly said. "and you shouldn't be making fun of it. No matter what it means, its a sin."

When we got home, I asked Mother what it was about a woman's legs that made folks lust and what exactly lusting was anyway. All we knew was that it must be bad.

"Were on earth did you hear something like that?"

"Out at Mrs. Neal's today when her and Mrs. Effie were fussing about how Mrs. Neal's shows her legs to everyone."

"Whatever were you thinking to go eavesdropping and putting your noses in other people's business?" She scolded.

"We weren't eavesdropping. We just overheard."

"If you weren't invited, you certainly were eavesdropping! Children, you must always guard your eyes and ears and be very careful of what you let them see and hear."

Then she told us the story about this nosy, gossiping child who was forever looking for stuff to talk about. Then one day snakes, lizards and frogs began leaping out of her mouth. She told us that what we see and hear will plant itself in our hearts and minds and that it would cause nasty things to grow on our tongues.

"You are responsible for what you see and hear so run from things that aren't good," she warned us.

It was Saturday and we were walking to the store with Mother. We would help her bring back a few groceries. She had built a fire in the cook stove when she realized she was out of several things. Most times she was busy during this part of the day so it was especially fun for us. It was something different, unexpected and exciting. We each got to talk with her and listen while we walked along. Her shining brown hair, held back with two long rhinestone hairpins, framed her beautiful face. She'd gotten them from her daddy on her fourteenth birthday. He had to work away from home but found the time to come and bring her this present for her birthday.

She looked just like a picture I had seen of Vivian Leigh in a "Gone With The Wind" poster. Her creamy complexion almost glowed. Her eyes were a crystal blue outlined with a darker blue. Her lips were perfectly shaped and her cheeks radiated a healthy pink glow. She was the most beautiful person inside and out. I loved the rhinestone pins about as much as she did. Maybe one day I'd get to wear them. These pins were special because she knew how difficult it was for her daddy to get off and come home. She only used them when she dressed up to go somewhere.

We came upon the main road where Luther Hinze rattled along. We all called him Uncle Luther. He was an old man who came to town riding in a goat cart selling soot rags, kindling wood and gourd dippers. Uncle Luther didn't have any legs. I don't know if he was born that way...if a war shot them off...if a doctor cut them off. All I know is he doesn't have legs. He will hop himself up over the sides of that cart with his strong arms then drop himself on the ground just walking on his hands. This surprises even those who have seen him do it many times. Everyone seems to stand at attention when he passes. He is like a hero of sorts as he comes and goes in that old goat cart. He's used to the stares. He just smiles at us and calls out, "Rags, kindling, dippers. Rags, kindling, dippers." He makes the dippers from gourds that he plants along his fence line. He does all he can to support that huge clan of children he and his wife have.

Mrs. Effie walked up and leaned her gossipy head, with its tightly knotted bun, over towards Mother's ear and said, "How can that stump father so many children? You know it's not him. Everyone has to know it's her fault. How can she show her face around here? It's a pure ol' shame and sorrow for her to waltz around barefaced and proud like she does."

I'd heard that babies came from storks. From cotton patches and sometimes even from up in the loft where Mrs. Effie said she had found hers. So I wasn't surprised that Uncle Luther had found babies from a stump or that the same stump could have that many babies in it.

Mother's mouth dropped open.

"Mrs. Effie, my children are present. Please watch your tongue. I swear there's no one who thinks like you do. Why I never would have even considered the matter."

"I didn't think so." She laughed. "You are always so naive, Madge

Brown. Get your head out of the clouds and pay attention to details."

"I don't think I need to be paying attention to the *details* that go on in other folks' lives. It's really not anyone's business. Now, if you will excuse me I need to get my shopping done. I need to get back to the house while my stove is still hot. Worrying about other people's details is a matter for the sad and lonely. Personally, I have too many of my own details to contend with. I certainly can't worry about anyone else's." Mother flounced off into the store.

I think Mrs. Effie liked to see Mother flustered because she brought it on every time she whispered to her. Mrs. Effie was always in the middle of something unpleasant. Anytime anyone was unhappy, uncomfortable, embarrassed or down right mad, Mrs. Effie seemed to be right in the thick of it. Clouds of carrion followed that woman everywhere she went. Folks who had known Mrs. Effie for ages say she has gossiped all her life. She would dig for gossip like one might dig for treasure. They say her first words were spoken to spread a rumor.

She walks around like an old black crow with eyes and ears wide open. If nothing worth interest flows into them, why she simply makes her up something to talk about. Something has to be said about somebody and it is her job to see that it is done.

On our way home it started to sprinkle. Levi Stokes came up behind us. He was driving the old tallyho wagon with the fringe out over the driver's seat. It swayed and danced over his head.

"Y'all hop in and I'll give ya a ride home. It's on my way and them groceries looks mighty heavy and it's starting to rain."

"Don't mind if we do," Mother said. "I hope we're not causing you any trouble though. It's nice not having to walk out in this weather. It came up all of a sudden."

"Well, I was just going down to Mr. Roberts' cow pasture to section off another part of the bullpen. Looks like ol' Domino won't be the top dog around here anymore. That mama cow had a bull this morning. Now we gotta have two bull pastures cause bulls don't get along too good."

"You mean there'd be a bullfight," Zeke said as he laughed.

Levi spit a stream of tobacco out the side of the wagon.

"You right 'bout that son. Why they'd plow in and lock horns with each other faster than you can say scat. It'd be a terrible thing to see. Course it'll be a while before it's needed. We get it ready soon as another bull comes cause we know we're gonna need it. Looks like this rain will get me out of work today."

"I sure am scared of that Domino. I hope this new one ain't as ornery," I said.

"Oh no, Miss Clair. Domino ain't nothing to be scared of. He acts all bad but he ain't as bad as he looks."

"You ain't scared of him?" Zeke asked.

"Naw. Not at all."

"Then you ain't scared of nothing," I said.

Levi just laughed as he said, "Yes, I am scared of something."

"What?"

"I ain't rightly sure what it is but it scared the living tar out of me. Um…hum. I sure was scared. I'm telling you the truth. I get scared just sitting here in this broad open daylight talking about it."

"How can you be scared of it if you don't know what it is?" Zeke asked.

"Well, I'll tell you what happened and you tell me if I should be afraid of it or not. The other night it was pitch black. There was no moon at all. I had my lantern lit on the seat beside me. I was going home and as I passed under the big chinaberry tree down near the fork I felt something heavy hop into the wagon. Right back there where you young'uns are sitting. I could feel its breath on my neck. I tell you, I was frozen stiff. I couldn't move. I couldn't turn around to look. All I could do was hold the reins and pray as I drove on. In a little while though I felt it leave. I took off as fast as this mule would go. Now tell me would you be scared?"

"Of course." We all agreed.

He pulled up at our cabin and helped us carry in the groceries. We ran inside to get out of the pouring rain. When he left he twisted the horseshoe upward. "You know y'all have your horseshoe turned the wrong way don't ya? When it's pointed down you're blocking your luck. When it's upward you're catching it."

From then on we were sure to watch that horseshoe. If it ever fell to where our luck was blocked we quickly turned it upright again.

Soon Daddy put two nails to hold it. He laughed. "Now that will keep the thing set right. I'm ready for all that good luck to pour in that's been blocked from that shoe hanging wrong."

That put our minds at ease.

Chapter Six

Tempted and Tried

THE first day of November brought sharp cold winds that coated the morning in a wonderland of crispy frost. We hurried along the path to school where the red-hot heater would have a blazing fire to warm our hands and faces. The spider webs that dangled along the way looked like glass sculptures glittering with frozen dew on their delicate frames. There seemed to be millions of them scattered about. "Look. There's a spider's crystal palace." I pointed. "It's beautiful." It was hard for me to think of these lovely forms suspended among the trees as the homes of creepy spiders.

"They do look like crystal," Shelly said as we emerged from the path onto Main Street and headed toward the red brick schoolhouse.

We were late, had missed the flag raising, and the Pledge of Allegiance. The flag's fluttering seemed to be urging us to hurry. We went inside and quickly hung our coats and hats on their hooks and sat down. I was glad to feel the warm room as I sat there listening to the teacher talking about some fellow by the name of Adolph Hitler. Seems as if he was doing some fussing and fighting with his neighbors and stuff. It was all too far away for me to worry about. I would let all the grown-ups tend to that. I would study my spelling before the test that I knew was coming. I had my speller propped on the desk looking for the words list page when Floyd, who was seated in front of me, reached back and snatched the book out of my hands. He suddenly threw it to the front of the room where it landed with a loud crash.

Mrs. Neal wheeled around from the blackboard. "Who threw that?"

I didn't want to be branded as a tattletale so I waited for Floyd to speak up. Nobody spoke up.

"Whose speller is this?" Mrs. Neal snapped. I put my hand up. "Come here and pick it up." She pointed her long instruction stick at the book. I bent over and picked it up. She swatted me. "Don't you ever, as long as you live, throw another thing in my classroom, young lady. You do this after I let you by with being late? Go stand in the corner."

I leered at Floyd as I blurted out, "But I didn't..."

"In the corner." Mrs. Neal propped one hand on her hip and shook her stick at me with the other. "Don't talk back, young lady."

I stood in the corner and swore that I'd get even with that hog-faced puke if it took the rest of my life. He was meaner than a rabid dog, uglier than a mashed fish head, and more stupid than a retarded jackass.

As I stood there wishing I could go home I thought about Bay. He'd always stand at the window watching us go off to school and wanted so much to come with us. I was glad he wasn't here with a teacher like Mrs. Neal. Goodness knows what Bay would do. I thought about his small face mashed against the dusty windowpane as he held the tin soldier that he and Zeke had played with that morning. We were all close and we'd sometimes beg Mother to let Bay come to school and spend the day with us, but she said school was for learning and not playing. I felt that we all belonged together like peanut butter and jelly. Now I was glad he didn't have to come here.

I started thinking of ways to get Floyd back. I knew what I would do. I would beat him out to the swing and would not give it up no matter what. It was nearly time for recess. I was already standing so I knew I could beat him to it. Floyd most always got the swing and hogged it. He wouldn't let anyone else near it. Even if someone did get to the swing first he'd just come over, take hold on the swing and say, "Get out."

Well, today I would defy him to make me give it over. I'd hang on and sit there no matter what he said. Even if he yelled, hollered or cussed, I wouldn't give it over. This would really wound him to the core that I would refuse to mind him. I had to bite my finger hard to keep the giddy laughter from escaping. I couldn't wait till recess.

When Mrs. Neal called recess I took off as fast as I could to stake and hold my claim to the swing. Just as soon as I got in it here he came making a beeline for the swing. He took hold of the ropes.

"Get out," he demanded.

Everyone stood watching as I sat there and said, "Make me."

Well, that was the worst thing I could have said to big, booger-lipped Floyd.

"If you're gonna sit there then I'm gonna swing ya."

He began pushing me higher and higher. As he pushed the limb would bounce, the ropes would squeak, and my body would nearly hang itself in the limbs and leaves. I screamed at the top of my lungs. I yelled. I kicked. The children ran to get the teacher. Floyd stopped the swing with a snap and dumped me hard on the ground.

"What's going on?" Mrs. Neal asked as she came rushing out the door toward us.

"I was gonna push Clair in the swing," he lied. "She didn't want me to so she lit into yelling, pulling away and carrying on so that she fell right out of the swing. I was trying to help her up, and she started screaming again. Stupid girl."

"I can't believe you'd tell such a lie!" I yelled as I jumped off the ground. It seemed I couldn't win for losing anyway and I'd had enough, so I kicked him as hard as I could right on his shin. He bent over crying and rubbing his leg.

I got another switching and he got the swing.

My anger knew no bounds. I hated Floyd. I hated Mrs. Neal for believing him and I hated school because Floyd was there. I began to plot other things to do to him…things that he couldn't wiggle out of. Try as I might, when it came down to it, I couldn't lie on him and all my best plots included a lie.

Eventually I gave up and tried to stay out of his way. That didn't work either. He was one of those who will hunt you down to start trouble.

One day he came up behind me on the playground and knocked my feet out from under me. I jumped up and tore into him like white on rice. I scratched. I kicked. I bit and I hit till I was so tired I could fight no more.

When I got through with that rotten ol' Floyd he was sitting on the ground, crying his eyes out, saying he wanted his Momma. Mrs. Neal came out to find him crying and me standing there with my hair falling in my face. A clump of Floyd's hair was in my still, tightly clenched fist. A very large smile showed no remorse on my dirt-covered face. I was totally and completely satisfied that he had finally got the whipping he deserved.

My joy was short-lived. Mrs. Neal turned me over right there on the playground and tanned my hide good. She sent me home with a note for Mother and Daddy. I was still happy that I had beat Floyd, but I was nervous about what punishment I would get for fighting at school.

On my way home I passed by Sadie May's place. She was outside in her turnip patch. Her sack dress spread over her bony hips and hiked itself above the backs of her knees as she bent over. She was snapping off the tender leaves while ever so often pulling up a purplish root. She had formed a long, deep pocket by drawing up the edges of her apron and holding it in one hand. She inspected the leaves for any obvious bugs or bad places before laying them over in the gathered up apron. Her black, nappy hair was tied up in a red scarf with blue dots sprinkled over it. She looked like a skinny Aunt Jemima with long arms jutting at the elbows like gnarly limbs. When she moved them they appeared to swing like twigs blown by the wind.

"Howdy do." She stood, put a hand to her back and arched it backwards trying to work out the kinks from bending over so long. Her belly poked out in front like a small cantaloupe. She waved at me. "Got me some turnips near big around as the water bucket. Won't take but a couple to make a nice mess." She walked toward the water pump. Her toes looked like turtleheads poking in and out of their worn shoe shells. The shoes had long ago lost any newness or shine but had a pretty good sole left. A blue jay screeched as it flew past and darted toward a fence post. "Noisy ol' jay-bird always a pestering and bothering the peace. Ain't never satisfied. Got to go 'round yelling all the time. Ain't never learned no song nor built no nest. Nasty ol' bird um huh, meaner than an ol' black crow in the cornfield." She trudged on. It looked like each step was measured, calculated and signaled from her brain. Slow, deliberate steps that did no hurt nor harm to the grasses that grew on the pathway.

"I thought all birds were sweet," I said.

"Oh no. Not even crows are so sweet."

"I'm talking about regular birds you know, like wrens, robins, sparrows, and those kinds. Not old buzzards, hawks, crows and stuff."

"I reckon about the sweetest bird on earth is the dove. It is God's bird."

"Did you ever see a dove?"

"Sometimes you can see one around. I saw a white one once."

"If you see a white dove it means good news and God is sending you a blessing. That's what Mother says."

"Pretty well could be true. I heard it said that the white dove is a bird of peace." Sadie May dumped the turnip greens into a washtub that waited under the pump. She took the jar of priming water and poured it in the top while she primed the old pump and sent water gushing over the greens. She filled the jar, replaced the lid and set it back down beside the pump. She went about sloshing and scrubbing the greens. "It's getting plumb chilly this time of year," she said. "I can already taste the Thanksgiving turkey."

"Yeah, and after that it's Christmas!"

"Have you been good this year? What you doing coming home so early and all by yourself?"

"I've tried to be good, but mean Floyd made me fight. He threw my speller, pushed me out of the swing and kicked me."

"My, my, it looks like he's wanting switches in his Christmas stocking. That boy is always getting everybody in trouble."

"I got mad and fought with him so I have to go home and take Mother and Daddy this note." I held it up. "I reckon I'll be getting old switches and stuff too."

"Not less you just lookin' for trouble being mean and pure out hateful. Floyd acts like a mean ol' bird. Is that what you wanna be? Looks like you're letting him pull you from a dove to a crow."

"I don't want to be a crow."

"Then take the note on home and welcome the chastising so you will grow up to be a sweet dove. You know, kind, gentle and loving? Floyd needs somebody to take a strap to his backside a time or two. You know what the Good Book says. A child left to itself brings ruin to the family. I don't expect you wanna be bringing no ruin to yours, right?"

"Right."

As I walked home I felt better about being punished. I didn't want to be like Floyd and I figured that he didn't want to be like himself either. Maybe he was like that Hitler fellow. Just outright power hungry and wanting everything for himself no matter who it hurt.

A little way down the road I passed by the Grangers' place. Mr. Granger came running out in nothing but his long handles and a hat. "Could you help me just a little?" He seemed frantic.

"Um, y-y-yes sir," I hesitantly replied. "What do you need?"

"I need more muscle than I've got, that's what I need. Can you help me? My wife's stuck beside the stove and I can't pull her up."

I followed him in the house and into the kitchen where Mrs. Granger's gowned behind and slippered feet were sticking up from between the stove and counter shelf. She was yelling for somebody to help her get up.

"The blood's gone to my head and my pure eyeballs are fixing to pop right out if somebody don't get me up from here!" We reached over and pulled her up by her armpits. When she got upright she began fanning herself and panting.

"What happened?" I wanted to know.

"I dropped my grit pot over there and tried to reach it. I lost my balance and went head over heels inside that hole. I have been needing a shelf or something over that corner hole. I have begged and begged Mr. Granger to close it off. But do you think he'll do it? No! He'll just go out in the yard and walk his blasted path till time to eat again."

They both thanked me kindly and gave me a nickel. I would stick the nickel in my Christmas savings jar to buy something nice for everyone come Christmas time.

When I got home and they read the note Daddy looked at me and said, "Let's go out to the barn young lady." I gladly followed him to receive my chastising. "You usually whine and try to get out of a whipping. What's the matter with you?"

"Daddy. I don't want to bring ruin to my family and I don't want to be like mean Floyd, so I am ready to take whatever chastising I deserve for what I did."

I meekly bent over and closed my eyes tight to ready myself for the fierce blow. But it didn't come. I looked back and Daddy had his back turned to me. I went over to him and laid my hand on his arm.

"Daddy. Are you awful mad at me? I am sorry."

He turned to me. "No Clair I'm not mad at you. I think you have learned your lesson this time so I won't whip you."

"Oh no, Daddy. I have to get my whipping. Because in the Holy Bible it says that a child left to itself brings ruin to the family. Please Daddy, don't leave me to myself!" My voice sounded almost desperate.

"Okay, Clair, bend over." Three light swats and that was it, but I felt better and I hugged Daddy and thanked him for not leaving me to myself.

"I love you Daddy," I said as he hugged me tight and we walked back to the house.

The next day at school Floyd was acting strange, not mean, just weird. He smiled and showed me his book. He had written on its side Floyd + Clair forever. He winked as he held it up. I was so upset I went straight and told the teacher.

"Floyd had my name on his book saying me plus him. I don't like him. Make him take that off his book," I pleaded.

"It doesn't matter," she said. "It doesn't make it true just because he wrote it down. Now go take your seat."

"But everyone will think I like him."

"Clair. I said go sit down." I walked away defeated again.

At recess Mary Lou and her friends skipped by singing, "Clair loves Floyd. Clair loves Floyd." Then I walked by him. He was in the swing again, but he jumped up and came over to me.

"Do you want to swing? I won't push you unless you want me to and I won't push you so rough this time."

"No, Floyd. I don't want to swing. I want you to leave me alone and get my name off your silly ol' book! I don't like you at all! You had no business putting my name on your book like I'm your girl."

"Clair, I'm sorry for all that stuff I did. Won't you be my girl?"

My skin crawled and I yelled, "No! Never! Not in a million years! Get away from me!"

"You're awful pretty and smart too. I like you. Why can't you like me?"

"I'll never like you. Never. I mean it Floyd, you'd better take my name off your smelly ol' book."

"Can't do that. I wrote it in ink. It'll be there forever."

Then of all things he started to pal around with Zeke. Before long he was coming over every Saturday to play with him. He would bring wildflowers that he had picked for me.

I told Zeke to stop hanging around him.

Zeke said, "Nobody likes him and sometimes I feel sorry for ol' Floyd. When you tore him up that just buttered my grits. I have waited for that piece of mess to get his just deserts ever since we first stepped foot in that school. You know what he told me? He said there was a picture of Betty Grable's legs on the wall of the bus station's toilet. I went to look and sure enough it was like he said. She seemed to be smiling right at me. I almost forgave Floyd for everything he'd done, and besides, it's better to be his friend than his enemy."

"Maybe it is for you but if that thing winks at me one more time I'll pass out from the pure humiliation of it all. He has a brain only a buzzard could appreciate. Rotted, you know, and I can't stand his stupid cross-eyed grin."

That Sunday Brother Paul made the announcement that he and Mrs.

Neal were getting married. Everyone gasped and stared at him like he'd lost his mind.

"Now. Calm yourselves down. I know there have been nasty rumors going around about this dear lady, but they're just that. Rumors. If Mrs. Neal made mistakes in the past, well, they are to be forgiven. Just as we ourselves make mistakes and must forgive each other."

Miss Effie's lips were as tight as her corset. I knew Mrs. Neal's ears would be burning and so would the preacher's. And sure enough she started running her mouth the minute she stepped off the church grounds.

"Our pastor is marrying the town slut. Don't that take the cake? Can you imagine? What will happen next I ask you? I knew there was something going on between them. But would anyone listen to me? Oh no. Brother Paul is going to be mighty sorry that he entertained that one. She's a trollop and nowhere near worthy to be the wife of a pastor. She'll ruin him and break his poor heart in the process. You mark my words, this will be a disaster the likes of which this town has never seen. That woman is nothing but a twisted web of confusion in gaudy attire. She's more than likely pregnant and trapped him into marrying her sleazy behind. If he can anchor her in the straight and narrow I'll say he has beat Goliath."

I couldn't worry about Brother Paul's Goliath. I had one of my own to fight. Floyd was forever trying to spark me. I didn't know how, when or where, but I would get that stupid Floyd out of my life. I would make him leave me alone in a way that wouldn't bring ruin to my family.

Chapter Seven

County Fair

It was Saturday noon and we were walking to the county fair. It had been put off several times because of heavy rains. Just as the ground would get nearly dry enough, lo and behold there'd come another gully washer. It had rained so much that the creek spilled over its banks and came creeping up to the cabins. It rose until it was right at our door. Another inch or two and it would be in the house.

We'd asked Daddy why the water was still rising even though it had stopped raining. He told us it was because of all the floodings up north of here.

"Those big rivers empty into these smaller rivers and creeks. But this is still not like the flood of '28. Even the mighty Mississippi cut a new route out as the gushing water whipped against the waiting banks. It even overtook the levees. I'm here to tell you it was one of the most awful floods this country has ever witnessed. All the townspeople and plantation workers along these river towns worked nonstop shoring up these levees, but Greenville's wound up breaking anyway. A lot of workers were just swept away right then and there. Others took off running like a sudden gust of people pushing along the length of the crumbling levee. Many towns and homes were completely destroyed. Most all of the people and plantation workers left that part of the country. I don't think they ever came back. Too much heart ache, pain and loss."

Mother dunked the mop in the high water outside to rinse it. "This is the world's biggest mop bucket." She laughed as she wrung the mop out.

Finally, the rains had stopped. The ground was dry and the fair was here. We had been anxious to get there since early morning. Mother told us we could go ahead of them. She and Daddy would come later.

Ol' Blacky danced at our heels acting like he was as excited as we were. The Grangers pulled alongside us in their old gray pickup. "Where y'all headed?" he asked as he poked his head out.

"We're going to the fair," Zeke answered.

"That's where me and Mama are going. Hop over in the back and we'll take you there."

We knew Mother and Daddy would beat the whey out of us if we crawled in that truck with Mr. Granger at the wheel. They didn't trust his driving. In fact nobody in these parts trusted him to do much of anything.

"No. But thank you just the same. We want to walk."

"Y'all ought to ride with us. It's pert near a mile to the fair," Mrs. Granger said.

"It's all right. We're used to walking."

"Okay, then. If y'all get time come by the exhibits and see how my peanut butter cake made out."

"Oh, we'll be there. We have a few things in the judging too."

"Wouldn't be a cake now would it? I know your Mama makes some of the best ones in the world."

"No, ma'am. We didn't enter a cake."

"Good, good! Well, we'll see y'all at the fair."

As the truck pulled away we looked at each other. "Peanut butter cake? Can't you just imagine how good that's gonna taste?" Shelly grimaced. "Mrs. Granger is weird as they come."

"She'd have to be to be married to Mr. Granger but she's goodhearted and funny. I like her."

"I like her too." Shelly began to laugh.

"What's so funny?"

"I was just thinking about the time we were trying to learn how to stand on our hands and as we passed her place she was on her porch watching us."

I laughed along with Shelly as I remembered what happened. Mrs. Granger had yelled out to us, "Come over here and I'll show y'all how it's done." We walked up on her porch. "If y'all would use the wall of the house to keep from falling it would be easier. You can't fall that way. I'll show y'all how to practice." She went in the house and put on a pair of Mr. Granger's overalls and told us to stand back and watch. "Y'all watch close and learn." She did the flip all right but one of her legs went through the wall. We worked feverishly to get it loose while she hung upside down and hollered until we got the leg prized loose. She rolled over on the porch looking to see how bad she was hurt.

Mr. Granger came upon the porch from his thinking path.

"What in the name of Christmas are y'all up to? I thought for a minute there that I was seeing myself. What are you doing wearing my pants, Mama? Don't no woman supposed to wear no man's pants. You look plumb ridiculous."

"Not nearly as ridiculous as I looked a few minutes ago with this house hanging off of my leg. Help me up and let's see if I can walk." She sat on the porch with her leg propped on a milking stool. Her twisted toes poked up in the air. She was forever stumbling against the furniture and anything else that shared the same floor space with her feet. She'd broken every toe on both feet and now they were numb, twisted lumps. She'd bang into things with nothing more than a grunt. "I was never meant to have toes," she'd say, "because it wasn't till after I broke them all that I could walk straight." She had laughed.

"Yeah, I remember her toes looked like short little corkscrews all poking up from her feet." Zeke said. We all laughed as we hurried on down the road toward the fair.

"Hey, wait up!" Maxine called as she ran toward us. "I'll walk with y'all. I have my jam in the exhibits. Y'all got anything?"

"Yeah, Shelly has her embroidered mantle scarf and Mother has her pickles."

Before long we could see the booths, tents and barn down in the pasture. The loud music playing made our feet move faster to get there. The square dancers were kicking up sawdust that had been hauled in from the sawmill to cover the fairgrounds.

We walked through and passed a booth where an old black woman sat. Her sign said she could remove warts. We all looked for a wart because we wanted to see it removed. Nobody had one so we walked on.

A man put a chicken to sleep. He put its head under its wing and rocked it. Then he put it on the ground where it lay still as death until he woke it up.

A woman picked up a chair with her teeth and held it straight out in front of her.

A farmer sat beside one of the biggest pumpkins we'd ever seen. He called it Peter's Pumpkin.

Mrs. Neal was there with some of her concoctions. Her big hit was the whole pears inside glass bottles. Everyone was amazed and wondered how she squeezed a whole pear through the tiny neck of those bottles.

We passed the cake exhibit. There. Right in the middle of two of the most delectable cakes: *Chocolate Dream* and *Coconut Fantasy*...Mrs. Granger's Peanut Butter Nightmare. She didn't call it that but we did. It looked even worse than it sounded. She had it iced with peanut butter and sugar and had named it *Peanut Butter Cream*. It looked like a light brown cow pile. I didn't envy the judge's job of tasting that one.

In the sewing exhibit, Shelly's mantle scarf had won a blue ribbon. She was forever finding some reason to go back to the exhibits so she could look at her ribbon again. "I know you can sew Shelly, but I want to do something else besides stare at your blue ribbon while we're here," Zeke said.

"Yeah. Maybe when you get it home we'll all sit around and look at it more, but right now there's so much more to see." We walked on and saw a tent with nothing but a long scarf-like ribbon blowing in the wind. It was tied to a pole beside the tent and fluttered and waved. "That's strange. Nobody's here...just a piece of cloth blowing around. I wonder what that's here for?"

"I don't know. Maybe this is an empty place waiting for someone to come and run it."

"Come on. We'll stop by later and see what it is."

Just then the flap opened and there stood a tall gypsy woman with her finger held over her mouth shushing us. She had on a purple turban sprinkled with yellow stars and yellow quarter moons on her head. A long, purple cloak draped around her shoulders and reached down to her yellow, pointed shoes that glittered like gold in the sunlight.

"Be awful quiet," she said. "Come inside to where the crystal ball is speaking."

Her wide eyes stared at us. We followed her inside the tent to where many candles flickered around a table holding a large crystal ball that glowed above a deep blue tablecloth. The gypsy gazed at it a minute and then looked at us. "It talks about four children," she said. "You four children. If you want to hear what the spirit in the crystal ball says you must put a nickel on the table." Her mouth was pursed, her eyes circles of glaring light as she twisted her long fingers over the ball.

Zeke was first to get to his nickel and he plopped it on the table.

"What's it say?" We stared at the mystical ball.

"The magical clouds show me that you four children will receive a reward in the very near future. A nice big one."

"You mean besides my blue ribbon?" Shelly asked.

"Yes. This reward is for all of you. A big reward."

That was just about the best fortune we could have had. We considered our nickel well spent as we walked through the sawdust midway looking at everything and listening to the music. Daddy was up on stage with his fiddle and all the other musicians from around the county. We watched the dancers as we clapped and jumped to the cheerful music.

Floyd came up behind us and tapped me on the shoulder and yelled over the music, "Would you dance a reel with me Clair?"

"No! Get away from me you bugger-lipped leach!" I shoved him as hard as I could.

He came back and gave me a quick peck on my cheek and ran into the crowd.

I wiped my face and screamed after him. "I hate you! I hate you forever and always!" I grabbed my dress sleeve and wiped and wiped where he had kissed me and yelled again. "I hate you! Do you hear me?"

We noticed Joe Blass up there with the rest of the musicians. He was dressed fit to kill and plunking on his guitar like all get out. We thought he looked real nice up there tapping his foot to the music like he'd always been sober.

"That's the first time I've ever seen ol' Joe in his right senses."

Daddy stepped off the platform and went over to Mother. He bowed and asked her to dance. They were the best around and everyone was impressed.

As they danced the hoedown the floor was cleared so everyone could watch. Their fast-moving feet whipped the sawdust into a flying frenzy as onlookers clapped in time with the music. Before long they had added a little of the Charleston along with the Black Bottom to the reel. Now that was something to watch.

When they were through Mother was out of breath. Daddy went to get cool drinks for us all. Then we walked around the midway looking at everything. We watched the expanding crowd. People had come from everywhere. There were old, middle-aged, young, and children of all ages. Still, more came. People stood in groups talking and eating while little ones crawled through the forest of legs.

They announced the taffy pull. There would be two people in each team competing to get the taffy pulled the quickest. Me and Shelly wanted to do it so we entered. As everyone stood waiting they came by with butter to put on our hands and then laid a glob of hot taffy in them. We began to pull. Shelly and I had a secret to pulling taffy. She would hold it and I would run out and run back before it hit the ground then Shelly would run out and back. The crowd cheered for us.

"Look at them! Now ain't that about the best way you ever seen to pull taffy? That's smarts. That's called using your noggin."

Other teams tried to copy but they didn't know the exact knack of it and their taffy hit the ground and got full of sawdust. We won the taffy pull and our prize was the taffy. They rolled it into a long strip and cut it into little blocks then rolled it in wax paper and bagged it for us then pinned a big blue ribbon on the bag. That evening when we were on our way to the exhibit building to pick up Mother and Shelly's entries, ribbons, and our lantern, Floyd came running up with the sweetest little Kewpie Doll.

"Here, Clair. I won this for ya."

I wanted that Kewpie Doll with all my heart. She was so beautiful with her little fat arms and legs and her round little smiling face with that little topknot just set it off. But I didn't want to take it from that putrid, ugly boy. Mean Floyd, the ugliest thing in the world, was standing there offering me the cutest thing I had ever seen.

"I don't want it." I told him coolly "Shelly might. Ask her."

Oh, how I hoped he'd give it to Shelly, so we could share it. I looked at her begging as hard as I could with my eyes to take the doll from him. I jabbed her in the side with my elbow. "He won it for you, Clair."

"Well, I don't want it. I don't want anything from the likes of him." I punched Shelly again, and whispered, "Get it. We can both have it."

Shelly stepped up. "Give it to me and I'll give it to her." She put her hands out.

"No!" Mean Floyd jerked it away from Shelly. "Clair has to take it from me because she's my girlfriend. You're not."

"I am not your girl." And with a regretful heart I said, " I don't want that stupid doll. She's too fat and made of hard chalk anyway. You take that doll and get away from me. I don't want anything you put your nasty hands on."

We all walked on as Floyd followed a little ways behind singing, "Ca-Ca-Ca-Clair-ee you beautiful Clair-ee, you're the only ga-ga-girl that I adore." He followed us singing that song until we met up with Mother and Daddy at the exhibit building. Then he ran off tossing the doll in the air and letting her hit the ground over and over as he went.

"I wish that doll would come down on top of his head and brain him," I said to Shelly as we watched him go.

"You should have took it from him, Clair. He's just breaking it all up when we could have had it."

"I hate him. I hate him so much, Shelly. If I had taken it from him then he would really think I was his girlfriend."

"He really thinks it now, Clair. Nothing would have changed."

"Yeah. But if I had taken it he would have had reason to think I was his girlfriend. As long as I know I'm not and everyone else knows he's just acting crazy I don't care."

"Yeah. It really sounds like you don't care," Shelly said. "You're always up in the air about it. Me think thou doest protest too much." She laughed

"Shut up, Shelly. You're being mean now. You're mad cause he wouldn't give you the doll."

We walked home as the booths were closing and the lanterns were lit. The night muffled the voices around us. Daddy swung the lantern as he and Mother walked ahead. Mother pointed. "Look at that moon. It looks like a Harvest Moon."

A huge orange moon rose above the trees. The roosting chickens cooed from the limbs of a nearby chinaberry tree. Crickets chirped and a far-off whippoorwill cut through their steady humming. The trees and bushes looked scary. A screech owl screamed.

Shelly stopped in her tracks. "I hate that sound. It makes my skin crawl and my hair stand on end."

"It's only a screech owl. If you turn your pocket inside out and twist it that'll break his neck."

"How do you know?" She pulled at her pocket.

"Because. That's what you do to keep them from making more witches."

As Shelly frantically twisted her pocket she said, "We read a book at school about birds and owls and it didn't say a thing about twisting pockets."

"That's because witches wrote that book. They don't want everybody to know how to kill screech owls. They'd kill all of them and there wouldn't be no more witches."

"You ever killed one?"

"Yeah, I reckon I have. I've been knowing how to kill screech owls for a long time."

"You think I killed that one?"

"Did you twist your pocket tight?"

"Yes."

"Then you killed him. But you gotta be sure you kill them by twisting your pocket good and tight. If you don't kill them but just hurt them, it makes them awful mad."

Suddenly a loud yell split through the night air.

"It's the screech owl's ghost or the witches are mad at us for killing that screech owl!" Zeke yelled as we took off running to catch up with Mother and Daddy.

Everyday after the county fair we waited and watched for some wonderful reward.

"That old gypsy took our nickel." Zeke said. "We didn't get a reward of no kind."

"Maybe she meant the taffy."

"But she said a nice big one."

"The bag was big and we all ate it."

"Yeah, and it was nice!" Bay laughed.

After a while we forgot about the old gypsy woman and her predictions.

Chapter Eight

In the Gloaming

NOW that the fields were picked clean and the vegetables canned and ready for the winter months, the quilting bees began. These bees would last from the wee hours of the morning until late evening. Whoever would host the quilting that day would cook up plenty of food and stack it on the safe, the stove and the table. It was like having a picnic inside the house. Little ones played underfoot while babies nestled in beds or dangled across their mothers' laps. Women laughed, talked, and stitched the artful quilt.

Sometimes an older girl stayed home from school to help with the babies and learn the many different stitches. I could do the slipstitch, lock stitch, birds-eye, overcasting and straight stitch. Shelly had mastered more than I had. She liked all kinds of sewing from quilting and embroidering to darning. She could make some of the tiniest and neatest stitches that anybody had ever seen. "She's just a natural born seamstress," folks would say as they looked at her work. "Nothing but maybe a Singer could beat her."

Mother would get up at 3:00 a.m. to finish her chores, cook breakfast, and wash the dishes. Then she'd tie on her hat and shawl, take her sewing basket, and walk to the bee. The women would sew until around twelve o'clock when the men folk came sifting in to eat dinner. Afterwards there would be naps and two o'clock coffee before returning to the quilt. Late that evening the quilt would be finished and draped over the bed. We enjoyed these times because we could meet with our friends after school wherever the bee was that day. We'd play until Daddy and the other men came in at dusk to eat supper.

We'd ride home bundled in the back of the wagon. The dark night closed around us as we rode toward home.

"There's no moon tonight," Zeke said.

He started talking about the *thing* that had jumped into the tallyho wagon when there was no moon. We all pushed closer together.

"Be quiet Zeke. You'll scare Bay," Shelly said as she looked around and scooted closer into the huddle.

"But it's true. The thing was breathing right on his neck."

"If you say another word I'm going to tell on you. Talk about something else."

Zeke liked to be scared and he liked to scare us. The more eerie the story the better he liked it. Or maybe he was just scared and trying to get us to tell him it would be all right.

On cold evenings we'd sit by the fire listening to the men folk spin yarns. Mother sat in her rocker with her sewing basket beside her patching and mending things that could be salvaged. She cut other items into odd shapes for scraps to make quilt tops.

We were still sleeping under a quilt that Granny had made when she was a little girl. Many nights we'd fallen asleep listening to Mother telling the history behind each square. These history quilts and their stories gave me a warm secure feeling about the world and my place in it. The blue blocks sprinkled with small white flowers came from one of Grandma's best Sunday dresses. The yellow squares are from the dress she wore to her first spring fling. She danced in the middle of the street with Grandpa. He was fourteen and she was twelve. The plain white cotton squares are from Great Grandpa's shirts and the green ones from Great Grandma's housedress.

During these cold evenings we'd watch the fire and listen to the rhythmic creaking of Mother's rocker as the men folk talked. They told tales and tried to outdo each other. The one who could tell the best yarn was honored and admired. James Stokes was usually the center attraction because of his far-fetched stories he declared true, seen and witnessed, as he'd say, "by my very own eyeballs."

One cold moonless night he folded his tall frame in a straight-backed chair in front of the fireplace. He shoved an ample wad of tobacco in his jaw and began his elaborate tale. "Now y'all know about how us black folks come over here from Africa, right? That's where they practice stuff like voodoo, hexing and rituals of all sorts. Well, last week on my way home from over here I passed by Mable Lee's. I heard her just a chanting up a storm. Now usually I stay away from things like that, but that night I felt like I should look in and see what was going on. I mean, since I do know a little about such stuff."

I scooted closer feeling the excitement. I knew some eerie tale was coming up.

James wound his long legs around the chair, poking his feet on the rungs and continued. "I've been all over creation. Heard a lot and seen a lot. But this here chanting was the strangest sounding stuff I'd ever heard. My hair stood up on my head and I sidled up to the window to get a closer look. Mable's black face was shining like a new greased wash pot. She twisted her head like the agitator on one of them there Sears and Roebucks washing machines. That wad of rings in her ears jingled and slapped against her big neck. She had a flat round hat balanced on her head like a platter. I knew she was chanting up some spell so I listened.

"I heard her say, 'Tonight exactly at the midnight hour the screech owl screech and give the power.' I mean to tell y'all it was all I could do to keep from running away from that window. I'd put myself there to find out what was going on. I wanted to know and I thought y'all would want to know too, so I just craned my neck forward and kept on looking and listening. Hex stuff hung all around and danced in the lamplight. Suddenly she called out, 'Lilac Rose, Lilac Rose,' which is her daughter, you know.

"Her lanky girl come shuffling out of a room and asked, 'What you want Mama Mable?' The girl had her hand propped on her hip and looked aggravated about being disturbed from whatever it was that she was doing.

"Mable Lee said, 'I need turn loose the power tonight and you the one stands to get it.' I do declare she said those very words, and I'm here to tell you I was near scared white. I could feel all the blood drain out of my face as I stood there. I sure enough was ready to get on away after that but I figured I owed it to you folks to find out everything I could.

"The girl told Mable Lee that she didn't want no hexing powers. She said if she ever got any such powers that honestly, she'd wring L.Z.'s neck like a skinny chicken's. The girl shook her head and seemed to be thinking strong about something. Then she said, 'You see him cry and cuss and be damned if he gonna cause me more trouble. He say he ain't never gonna stay out late no more and he be just a sweet-talking me into believing it. He say he be damned if he gonna touch anymore moonshine. Tears wash down his face like white lightning wash over the ground where he pour it out at. Now, he late again. I know he be drinking. My head get all fired up and I done killed L.Z. before I come to myself if I get hexing powers.'

"I watched her begging and Mable just a shaking her head and declaring that she'd have to take it. 'Tonight the night of the screech owl's screeching and the power gotta be passed on. You my child and gotta take it,' Mable said.

"'But what about I don't want it?' The girl stomped her foot.

"They kept on arguing. I listened to them a while longer fussing about passing on the power and stuff like that and then I walked on home. Just as I was crawling into bed I heard the screech owl. Its long screeching yell was louder and longer then any I'd ever heard in all my life. I was near frozen in my tracks. I looked at the clock and it was exactly midnight."

James leaned forward, spit in the fire and pulled a paper out of his hip pocket. "Feast your eyes on this."

He held up that very next day's paper. He said he'd been saving it to prove his story. There it was in black and white. We all read it. "L.Z. Ray, given name Lazarus Zachias, was found this morning hanging from the Sweet Gum Bayou Bridge. He was thrown from his truck and caught by the neck on one of the railings where he was hung and instantly killed. His neck was wrung like a chicken's."

Everyone stared at the newspaper account and declared that James was hard to beat when it came to telling tales.

As we were saying goodnight and everyone trickled out the door a hobo came by. He said he would work for just a pone of cornbread and maybe a little dob of pot licker to wet it down with. His clothes were loose and worn. He needed a shave and he smelled like stale wet hay. I'd heard tales of hobos and their adventures, but I'd never seen a real one before. I was hoping he could stay.

"We can't afford to take on another mouth to feed but you are welcome to a handout. In the morning you can talk to Mr. Roberts, who owns this place, about working for him. He can always use another hand."

"Thank you ma'am, but no ma'am, I don't want to get all tangled up in anybody's clutches. I got a home in Georgia."

Mother handed him a plate of leftovers.

"I wish there was more," she said. "If you think you need more I can stoke up the fire and fix you something else."

"No ma'am. I expect this'll be enough till morning. Thank you kindly till you're better paid." He sat on the steps with the plate on his knees and nearly inhaled the food. He sopped the plate clean as a whistle. "Do you mind if I sleep in your shed tonight?" He handed the empty dish back through the door and wiped his mouth on the sleeve of his dirty shirt.

"Go right ahead. I can't let you have a lantern though. We're nearly out of coal oil."

"I understand. Thank you anyway and I'm much obliged to you."

As he walked off Mother looked at me and shook her head. "So many folks out of work prowling around and hoping to find something better on down the road, yet there's nothing there…just more of the same or even worse. Folks are starving. Lord knows this depression is liable to kill us before it's done. It's attached itself to the world like a giant leech. The rich get richer and the poor get poorer."

I'd heard about the little match girl freezing to death and the little newspaper boy found dead with his head resting on a stack of his unsold papers and covered with one. This was happening in the big cities up north. They say the winters up there are much colder than ours where many orphans live in the streets. I couldn't imagine living in the street. I couldn't imagine anything colder than this cabin in winter.

Mother stuck her finger to her tongue and quickly felt of the kettle. It had been sitting on the leftover heat from the stove wood. "I hope he finds what he's looking for." Mother set the dishpan on the table and poured the water from the kettle into it. "We just can't hardly make it ourselves."

She washed the plate, put it in the safe and took down the clabbered milk. She skimmed off the thick yellow cream and put it in the churning crock along with the milk she would churn into butter.

We were disappointed because we couldn't have our very own hobo. We knew most everyone was having a hard time so we didn't put up any kind of an argument for him.

Zeke took a glass full of leftover clabbered milk, stirred in some musky dine juice and began eating it. "Before I pour the rest of this clabber in the slop bucket, go see if that hobo would like it, Zeke. And Clair, you take him that old quilt off the top of that trunk on the back porch."

We went out to the shed. It was getting colder and the hobo was gathering limbs for a fire that he'd started outside the shed door.

"Do you want some clabbered milk?" Zeke held the glass toward him.

"Yes, much obliged and thank you kindly."

I handed him the quilt while he and Zeke sat on a log in front of the fire and ate that nasty clabber. I couldn't believe anybody else on God's green earth would eat clabber.

"Listen to how that old north wind is blowing over the fields and through the trees. It sometimes sounds like somebody crying doesn't it?" He loudly slurped and scraped at the clabber with his spoon.

"Is it exciting being a hobo?" We wanted to know.

"This is about as exciting as it gets…something to eat and a warm place to sleep. I'm always alone except when somebody like y'alls family decides to pay attention to a body in need. I guess it's been months since anybody cared to talk with the likes of me. I mean like folks, you know. I do talk to the animals and such. A hobo is mighty lonesome."

"Have you always been a hobo?"

"Why are you one, anyway?"

"If you don't like being one, why don't you stop?" We bombarded him with questions.

"This is not by choice but by necessity. Things were so bad that I didn't know what else to do. I left my family in Macon, Georgia, while I went scrounging around looking for work. I left home in May while the first spring flowers were blooming. I expected to be home before they wilted. I've been all over the southland and haven't found the first bit of work. I reckon I could gather my family and move into this place and try sharecropping, but they tell me that when you get caught you'll never get loose from it."

Zeke and I looked at each other. We wondered if we had 'been caught'.

The next morning when Mother went to milk Ol' Brownie the quilt was neatly folded and placed on top of the hay pile. The hobo was gone.

Mother said, "I hope he finds what he's looking for. We should all pay attention to those in need because they could be angels unaware."

"What are angels unaware?"

"Angels that look like people…poor people, sick people and old people. So be mighty careful how you treat folks."

"Maybe he was an angel and had to go but I wish he'd stayed."

"Well, you couldn't look at him and tell if he was one or not," Zeke said.

"My goodness. If he was an angel then he knows about everything we've ever done."

"The worst thing we ever did was take those bird's eggs out of their nest and accidentally drop them."

"What about the time we switched those babies? And at a church house too."

We had gone with James to watch him play a trick on the church members. We'd help him by keeping the babies asleep.

It was on a warm night in early August that the Holiness Church was holding one of its all night revival meetings. We sneaked down the hollow and across the may haw slough to where the old knotty pine church sat nestled in a grove of loblolly pines. We listened to the yelling and lively spiritual dancing that went on. The commotion would carry for miles. We had waited until it was good dark so we wouldn't be seen and the meeting would already be in full swing. Lanterns hung from the rafters and from the trees directly outside the church. The doors had been propped open and we could see inside to where the shouting and dancing was going on. We watched from the shadows while their growing echoes vibrated through the trees. The trucks, buggies and wagons had quilts and blankets spread in them for the sleeping little ones. Every time they brought out a sleeping baby and laid it down, James would pick it up and trade it with one in another vehicle. If it woke up we had to pet it back to sleep.

Sometime during the long night the meeting ended and the tired worshipers went home. They saw the sleeping bundles and supposed everything was fine. This wound up being a bigger dither than any of us could have thought. Some travelers had stopped by to hear the gospel being preached. They were on their way to Memphis and their baby boy was left here. In its place was one of Sadie May's twin girls.

Church folks met down in that hollow for a while trying to get those babies traded back. We never told anyone about that night. There were some mighty angry parents who wanted to know who could have done such a thing and what they would do to them if they ever found out.

"Well, if he was an angel he knows how sorry we were about that. It wouldn't have been such a big thing if it hadn't been for those folks who were traveling," Zeke said.

We went to the shed, climbed in the loft and handed down the cow feed for Mother. She would pour it in the cow's trough before beginning to milk her. The cold wind moaned as it rattled the shed doors and pushed through the cracks. I scooped up a can of feed and thought about the wind being angel's wings. They were making the windy noises. I wished I could see a real one with long beautiful hair and shining wings…an angel with long flowing robes and glowing light around her gentle features. Could I dare to touch such a wonderful creature if she did appear?

Mother leaned against the cow's side, reached the udders and sent warm sweet milk hitting the pail with a ringing sound. I smelled its sweetness from the rising steam.

Winter was coming.

Chapter Nine

Japanese and Winter Freeze

WINTER came blasting through the Delta like a raging lion. The cold north wind howled and groaned around the corners of the house. It whistled through the chinked cracks as we huddled around the fire listening to James telling his tales. Tonight he said that there was something loose in these parts.

"I talked to Mr. Granger who said he had seen it. He said it was as tall as a man and as hairy as a wolf. He'd heard his chickens squawking and having fits so he had gone out there. He found chicken parts and bloody feathers strewn all over the place. It looked like something had ripped them apart and eaten them raw. Every night after that Mr. Granger would go out by the chicken yard with his gun and wait half the night trying to catch it."

James narrowed his eyes and continued the tale. "Last night around twelve o'clock he heard the thing coming back. It was making loud grating sounds like an elephant blundering through the woods tearing up saplings and underbrush as it came. He trained his gun in the direction of the noise and began backing toward the house. Suddenly the thing pounced into view and gave a blood curdling scream."

James let out a shrill yell and everyone jumped.

Mother hit him with a dishrag. "Quit scaring the daylights out of everybody James, you know Mr. Granger isn't all there. I shudder at the thought of him sitting anywhere with a gun. None of you kids needs to be afraid of any *thing* out there roaming around except maybe that shell-shocked critter with a gun."

James continued the story. "Well, Mr. Granger saw it and he pretty well knows what he sees. Don't you think? He told me that it had gone leaping away, scaling the fence in a single bound, then ran into the woods with several of his squawking chickens. He said it stood upright and was covered in long black hair. I bet that's the same thing that jumped into the tallyho wagon with Uncle Ned that night. There is a thing on the loose and it yells like a banshee."

The next day we were at the general merchandise store where the men folk sat huddled on the long benches out front. They talk over everything from weather to world situations.

Mr. Roberts was smoking his rosewood pipe and whittling. "What are y'all up to?" He held his pipe and scratched the side of his cheek with the stem. "Got money burning a hole in your pocket, huh?" He laughed. He saw me looking at the piece of wood in his hand. "This here's a gee-haw whimmy-diddle." He pointed out the notched stick with a propeller on one end. "You tell it which way you want it to go." He rubbed a small block of wood along the notched side and the little propeller twirled. "You say gee for right, and haw for left." The propeller twirled like a storm-blown windmill.

"Gee," I said, and the propeller paused, jerked to the right and speeded up again.

"Haw," Zeke said, and it spun back to the left.

"How did it do that?" Shelly said.

We were all pleased and puzzled.

"Well, it's the magic that does it."

Joe Blass came raveling down the road pointing toward the tracks. "I just seen that thing squatting down yonder on the railroad tracks." His unsteady hand shook.

"Well, maybe the ghost train will come along and run over it," Mr. Roberts said.

Everybody laughed.

"What's that you got there?" He slopped up the words. Mr. Roberts showed him the gee-haw whimmy-diddle and he watched it changing directions at every call. "Well, rip my drawers and call me tatters if that ain't about the smartest piece of wood I've ever seen." Joe stumbled away shaking his head. "Gee, haw. Now it sure enough does that."

We went in the store and bought ten sticks of licorice. We would each get two and a half pieces. We all, except for Bay, had ours gone by the time we reached home. Bay was so slow about eating. He had sucked the tip of one piece all the way home and still had all his candy. We watched him sucking and slobbering on that piece until we couldn't stand it anymore. At this rate it would be next week before he got it all down.

Zeke looked over at Shelly. "Hey, I know what would be fun. Let's play like we're the three little pigs and Bay is the farmer."

"That's no fun," Shelly said.

"Wanna bet? What about when farmer Bay has to feed his little pigs?"

"Oh, yeah." She laughed. "Let's build the pen right now. Clair, you and Zeke bring me four chairs." When Shelly got the pen built she told us to hop in and she did the same. "Now let's all crawl around and oink really loud."

We hadn't oinked more than three times when Bay came running. "I want to play too."

"We're playing the three little pigs, Bay. If you get in there'll be four. It wouldn't be right. I sure do want you to play though." Shelly looked sad.

"I know!" said Zeke. "Bay can be the farmer!"

"Yeah!" said Bay. "I want to be the farmer."

"If you're the farmer Bay you must take care of your three little pigs. You have to look after them. Your little piggies are hungry."

"Oink, oink. We're hungry Farmer Bay." We crawled around taking turns standing on our knees with our hands resting on the chairs and crying "oink oink, we're hungry" in front of Bay. He would offer his licorice strip and we'd bite off a piece. "Oh, thank you farmer Bay for taking care of us."

Before long his candy was all gone and the game was over. He cried. "I want to be the farmer again."

"We're tired right now. Maybe tomorrow we'll play again." Shelly told him.

I felt kind of bad about taking all his candy so I said I would play little pig with him. For hours I crawled around and oinked for Bay. He fed me paper, wood chips, leaves and anything else he could find while I pretended to eat them.

Zeke and Daddy cut wood and hauled it to the house. We picked up the last of the pecans, banked the potatoes and stored the winter vegetables, jellies and preserves in the shed. On these cold mornings Daddy built a roaring fire while Mother kept the stove red-hot with her cooking.

We raced from under the covers to the fire to get dressed. Sometimes it was so cold in the bedroom that we could see our breath and a layer of frost covered the quilts. The warm air carried the strong smell of perking coffee, fried salt meat, scrambled eggs and baking biscuits through the cabin. The hot breakfast, the thick winter clothes and new shoes kept us warm as we walked along the frozen road to school. We tried to stay on top of the wheel ruts because of icy water down inside them but the frozen ground caused us to slip and slide along. I couldn't keep my eyes off the shiny leather of my new shoes. My feet burned warm against their sturdy leather soles.

We had gotten them from the catalog store. Daddy had stood us up on a sheet of Blue Horse notebook paper and traced our feet. He sent these drawings along with the filled out order blank to the Sears and Roebuck's store. When the package came we sat anxiously waiting for Mother to tear into the thick, brown paper. The smell of new leather and the wonderful shine of the shoes sent our hearts leaping. We'd sleep with them hugged to our chest until the new wore off.

Right after Thanksgiving came Christmas preparations. At school we were learning how to make paper chains for the Christmas tree. We'd rush home anxious to show Bay how to color and paste these pretty chains.

Suddenly something dreadful and frightening happened during the joy and happiness of the Christmas season. The Japanese bombed Pearl Harbor, America's Navy base in Hawaii, and we were pulled into the war. It wasn't just out there somewhere. War was everywhere. Now there really was no end to hearing about the yellow slant-eyed Japs and evil demonic Hitler. Early Sunday morning on December the seventh these seething demons had reached out to trample a Godly and peace-loving nation…"the day that shall live in infamy" as Roosevelt had said. While they sacrificed to their heathen gods they attacked the country dedicated to the Almighty God of all creation.

Instead of stories by the firelight everyone talked about the war.

"Hitler is the anti-Christ," Daddy said. "He has six letters in each of his three names, 'Fuhrer, Adolph and Hitler'. The Japs are his little evil-eyed demons! I'm sure this will be our last Christmas on earth if we make it that far."

"Sure sounds right," James said. "Maybe this is the end of it all. But first I'm going to go kill me all the nasty heathen slant eyes I can get my hands on before I go. I think I need to send them on ahead, don't you?"

"I know how you feel, James. If I didn't have a family I'd go with you. All I can do is make this the best Christmas they've ever had."

Over the next days the invasion became less of a shock and more solid resolution by all of America. We would stand firmly together...we would stop this seething, evil monster in his raging desire to rule the world by using such demonic pawns. None of us could believe that the man our magazines had lauded as 1938's 'Man Of The Year' was this tyrant Hitler. And that he was the one controlling those mindless allies of his.

James had gone out and enlisted along with almost all the young men. The day he left we were so sad. Despite his tormenting ways we loved James. We would miss him.

Uncle Hank, who'd joined the U.S. Navy in 1938, had to go overseas. No one knew where he was and the only way to get a letter to him was to send it to a base in California. From there the Navy shipped it to him. His letters always came with a stamp that said it had "passed censor". He said that if we ever needed him in an emergency we should send a telegram. The Red Cross would get him home.

Grandma wrote that when he left she didn't want to seem afraid, or cause anyone to start bellowing, so she had stood by and quietly said her goodbyes. She said what she really felt like doing was screaming to high heaven and clawing the bus to pieces that took him. The letter had Mother wanting to go home. She worried so much for her brothers, for Grandma, and for everyone.

Mother and Boo tried hard to comfort each other.

"James will be home before you can say scat. Hank says that since America has joined the fighting it'll be over soon."

"James is a grown man but he's still my baby boy in a lot of ways. He ain't grown-up enough to see that kind of fighting. I wish I could have kept him from joining. He just wouldn't rest till he could get in this war. He's bloodthirsty…wanting to kill all the Japs he can for his cousin Leroy that was on the Arizona when it blew up. Soon as they can they'll send him on over there to fight. He won't never be the same boy that left here. I worry about him so much."

"Don't worry. He'll get through with God's help."

"Yeah. God's the only sure thing there is anymore this day and time. We always got Him," she said. "When you pray for your brother just add my boy in there too and I'll do the same for you and your folks."

"I already have." Mother placed a gentle hand on Boo's shoulder. "You're all in our prayers."

Over these fearful days everyone who could sew, bake, write or in any way help our soldier boys overseas went to work. Trains of solders came through town and most everyone went to greet them. We'd take cakes, cookies, sandwiches, tea and coffee.

We had heard that some of our boys were being brutally killed and maimed. Mother became jumpy and worried about Uncle Hank, her favorite brother and closest friend during her childhood. He had defended her, protected her and helped her through every crisis. Now he was gone to war. Who else in this world could she talk to about childhood memories like the both of them could? Her heart ached for him to be safe and to come home when this war was over. We found out that he had been sent somewhere out in the Philippines.

Every night after our usual bedtime prayer we would ask a special blessing for Uncle Hank, for James and for all the other soldiers who were in this bad war. Then suddenly there was Uncle Edward who had to be added to the special blessings list. He had up and joined the army.

Mother wanted to go home to be with her Mama and Daddy but she knew she couldn't. She cried a lot and prayed most of the time.

Daddy hung over the newspapers giving accounts of the depraved war dragon that was moving over lands like the plague and leaving destruction in his path. Men, women and children went fleeing from his wake like a surging wave from an angry ocean.

The cold wintry winds blew down from the North. Mother baked pies and cakes for Christmas and candies and cookies for the soldiers. In the evenings we'd sit in front of the fireplace shelling pecans and walnuts for the goodies.

The townspeople voted to decorate a tall cedar tree that grew beside the train tracks for the boys to see as they traveled on their way to the front lines. It could be seen for miles because of its gigantic height. Every evening the candles would be lit and hung on its branches by volunteers. We all wished to do something for those who would be leaving the comforts of home and Christmas.

This winter seemed to be much colder than any others. One evening Daddy opened the door and motioned for the Tailors to come in and warm up before continuing for their turn at the lighting of the tree. "Whoa there, Brother Clarence. You and Mrs. Grace come in and thaw out a bit."

"Don't mind if we do. Thank you very much." Mr. Tailor and Mrs. Grace walked over the ground and into the warm house. "It's cold enough to turn the fire into icicles."

Mr. Tailor hung his coat, hat and scarf on the coat rack and began helping Mrs. Grace get hers off and hung up. They stood in front of the fire warming themselves as they talked.

"I told Mr. Clarence it was too cold to walk to that tree but he wouldn't listen. He's just like a stubborn-headed mule. Stubborn-headed." Mrs. Tailor was a repeater. Everything she said had the tail of an echo.

"Now Mrs. Grace, I asked you right out if you wanted me to hook up the wagon and you said you wanted to walk."

"That I did but I had no idea it was so cold and when I found out I told you it was too cold to walk. Too cold. You said it weren't. You said it felt nice and crispy. 'Crispy, nippy weather', you said. That's what you said."

"Yes, I did. But it sure enough got a might dab colder since we left the house. In fact, I might ought to go on back and get the wagon." Mother brought in two steaming cups of coffee and handed them each one.

"Would y'all like a slice of rum cake?"

"Thank you, Mrs. Madge. It would be so good with this delicious coffee. Ain't nobody can make a rum cake as good as you do. But don't you go cutting it lest it's already been sliced. You hear? This here coffee is just what the doctor ordered. It warms me to my poor frozen toes. Warms me." Mrs. Tailor sipped on the coffee.

"Oh, it's fine. I wanted to sample it anyway." Mother went back to the kitchen and took down the rum cake.

Daddy shooed us out of the chairs and the Tailors sat down. "I'll hitch up the wagon and drive you there. I need to get a few things from the store anyway."

"Would you get me another bottle of vanilla flavoring?" Mother asked. "I've been forgetting it and finally ran completely out."

"Is that all you need?"

I knew that Mother also used the flavoring on herself. I'd seen her dabbing it behind her ears and inside her elbows.

I watched the Tailors amble out the door and into the cold night air. I shivered as a gust of winter wind swept though the open cabin door. I didn't know how they could stand to walk out in such weather. But then I remembered the time when they'd both nearly frozen because neither would pull down the window. It happened around Thanksgiving. Mr. Clarence was sitting in front of the fireplace while Mrs. Grace was cooking. She got a bit too hot and had raised a window. But Mr. Clarence had hopped up and pulled it down telling her he was about to freeze. She told him that he was dead and didn't know it if he was still cold after hunkering over the fire all day. They had fussed and fumed until he'd gone over and thrown the window wide open and neither would pull it down again.

I followed Mother into the kitchen where she began wrapping the cloths around her rum cake. She wet it down then put it back upon the shelf beside her fruitcake. As I stood watching her my stomach growled and we both laughed. She pulled it back down and cut me a tiny slice. "Don't go telling anybody," she said, "and don't go expecting another bite till Christmas. You hear?" She put the cake up. "Why if I didn't stop y'all we wouldn't have a single goodie for Christmas."

"I can't wait till Christmas. I can eat all I want then."

"Yeah, you can. And you can get a stomach ache and you can need a great big dose of castor oil."

I shivered from head to foot at the thought of that nasty stuff sliding down my throat and taking my breath away. I hated the smell of oranges when it wasn't Christmas time because that meant castor oil time. Ever so often, need it or not, there was this faithful dose of that horrible oil. As sure as rains fall and creeks rise castor oil remained in my life. I had to take the stuff. I would dream of vengeance on this pure ritual of torture. Somebody needed to hold Mr. Castor down and pour him full of his scummy oil. I wouldn't give that stuff to my worst enemy. Except for mean Hitler or Mussolini of course…those like that who go around hurting people and making war over the whole world. Somebody like that needs castor oil.

"There are nuts to be picked out." Mother put the cake up. "Let's get busy."

We went in and joined the others.

Christmas Eve came. There was going to be a gathering at the Baptist church for a worshiping service. After that everyone would gather around the big, lighted tree. We'd pray for our brave soldiers who couldn't be with their families on Christmas.

While we all stood in the light from the tree there was this great moment of silence because we knew why we were here. We knew at that very moment our boys were being fired on. Some would not return. Others would not look the same. But in that silence there was peace and resignation.

Boo clasped tightly to Levi's hand. In the glowing dull light I could see tears on Mother's cheeks. Quickly there came the most beautiful light streaming across the dark sky with a fiery glittering tail. It sailed straight from the east to the west over the beautiful tree of lights. Everyone gathered there, even the tiniest baby, made no sound or whimper. I knew that was for us all. This was a cold and magical night. The birthday of our Lord and He was with us. Then with a beginning soft hum the silence was broken as our voices gradually gave way to a rising chorus of "Hark The Herald Angels Sing".

I was proud to be a part of this wonderful ceremony. I watched the misty voices evaporate into the flickering candle lights and I heard some of the voices falter through the words of "Peace On Earth". I prayed for the fighting to end. I prayed for a joyous Christmas for everyone and for Santa Claus to come. The ceremony of praises ended with a soft verse of "Silent Night" then we all said our goodbyes and headed home. Tonight the candles would be left to burn themselves out because some would stay behind to watch them flicker their last dancing glow.

We huddled together in the wagon bed under thick quilts and watched the sparkling tree disappear into the distance. This had been a special evening and nobody seemed to have noticed the cold.

"I think that's the prettiest tree in the whole world," Shelly said.

"Yeah," I said, "it was worth all the trouble everyone went to." I put my hands over my ears and tried to block out the wind. I was the world's worst person for getting earaches and wind was cutting through my scarf.

"It was everyone's tree. That's why it was so special."

"It will always be special because of that bright light that flew over it."

"You reckon that light was Santa Claus?" Bay asked.

"I don't reckon so," Shelly said, "because he didn't even stop. But then again, maybe y'all have been bad."

"Well, he didn't stop for you either did he?" Zeke said. "So, what does that mean?"

"I reckon it means that it wasn't Santa Claus so we can all stop worrying about it, smarty pants."

When we got home we hurried through the door and stood in front of the fireplace while Daddy poked up the ash-covered embers and added logs to their red, glowing brightness. Soon the blazing flames leapt up to fill the fireplace and to warm our hands and faces. Daddy brought in a load of icy logs and laid them on the hearth. The frost glittering like diamonds in the dancing firelight sputtered and spit at the flames before slowly melting away. The assorted stockings dangling from the mantelpiece held notes pinned to each one saying "Dear Santa Claus". We had each made our letters of hope.

Shelly and I had asked for the Matilda doll like the one down at Mr. Grey's store. I'd heard Maxine asking Boo if she thought Santa might bring her one and Boo had said that it was really too much to ask Santa for. Now I was worried that I might not get her. I wanted that doll more than anything. It looked so real. It was made exactly like a real baby with a soft body and chubby little legs and arms. Her tiny mouth was slightly open showing two little white teeth resting against a soft, red tongue. She came with a baby bottle, a rattle, a bib and two diapers like real babies have.

Zeke wanted a big red wagon and Bay wanted a steel train that whistled and blew real smoke from its tall smoke stack.

We went to bed that night listening to the soft music gliding from the fiddle strings and for the pattering sound of reindeer on the tin roof. The music itself was like a gift because it had been so long since we'd heard Daddy play.

"Listen," Bay whispered, "I hear noises and it sounds like something scratching on the roof."

"That's probably a squirrel," Zeke whispered back. "Daddy is still awake playing his fiddle. It couldn't be Santa Claus. Daddy would see him."

"Oh yeah, that's right." He turned over and stuck his thumb in his mouth.

"You'd better stop that," Shelly said. "You know you're not supposed to put that thumb back in your mouth."

"It's Christmas. Let him have it," I said.

"Yeah, let Santa Claus see him. He'll bring him baby toys," Shelly said.

"I just kicked the habit forever," Bay said as he stuck his thumb behind his back. "I don't want Santa Claus to think I'm a baby. I want big boy toys. Especially that train engine."

Slowly the conversations drifted away and we were about to fall asleep when one of the loudest noises we'd ever heard swept throughout the countryside. We leapt up and ran with Mother and Daddy to the porch just as a wooden sleigh full of toys with Santa Claus at the reins was driving over the loose gravel into the yard. It was being pulled by a white stallion whose reins were filled with silvery, jingling bells. The Santa stood up and shouted "whoa" and pulled back on the reins as he laughed. "Ho, Ho, Ho!"

Clement C. Moor's Christmas story suddenly came alive right there in the sled dust of that dry, Delta gravel.

Mother turned toward us. "Oh, my goodness. Y'all are supposed to be in bed asleep. Hurry back in, quickly now before he sees you." She ushered us back into the bedroom and left the door slightly ajar where we all stood eyes wide and peering.

Bay began to tremble and whimper, "I can't see, I can't see."

Mother lifted him upon her hip. "Shush," she whispered. "Be very quiet. You don't want him to know you're still awake. If he thought y'all were still up he'd just go somewhere else until y'all were asleep."

"But didn't he see us out on the porch?"

"I don't think so. He was too busy trying to stop that sleigh."

Santa came in with a cotton sack flung over his shoulder. Daddy followed him, bringing two small chairs and a table. They looked exactly like the big ones he'd made for Mother except smaller and without a bench. He put them under the tree.

"I reckon these are for Shelly and Clair."

"Yes. They've been needing one for the tea set I left them last year."

Shelly and I looked at each other and smiled as we grasped hands and squeezed. I could see Shelly's eyes twinkling in the shadows of the dark room.

Santa had let the giant sack slip from his shoulder onto the floor with a muffled thud. "It's good having you help me this year. The elves are sick and Mrs. Santa is making them stay in bed wrapped in hot chest rags and sipping cocoa."

I felt sorry for the poor little things. I hated to be bound down in those awful chest rags. Mother would scorch them brown-hot from the iron then bind them over our rubbed down chests with a poultice of Vick's salve and oil. The vapors alone would nearly take our breath away.

Santa sampled the milk and cookies we'd left for him while Daddy went out and came back in pulling the brightest red wagon we had ever seen.

"Now, who is this for?" Daddy asked.

"I believed Zeke asked me for that."

I looked over at Zeke. His mouth was gaping and his eyes were fixed on that wagon.

Santa reached down into the sack and pulled out an iron train set.

"My train engine," Bay gasped.

"Shush, be quiet. Don't scare him away."

Bay clasped Mother around the neck and whispered, "He brought it Mother. He brought me a big boy train set."

My heart thumped hard against my chest. Bay and Zeke had gotten exactly what they wanted. Could there be a Matilda doll in that bag for me? I could feel my hand getting sweaty in Shelly's as Santa reached back into the sack and pulled out a Matilda doll. Everything in me rejoiced. She was more beautiful than she'd been in the store. I wanted to run to her, grab her and squeeze her to my heart.

But I froze as Daddy said, "That must be Shelly's doll."

My heart sank. I wanted to cry and scream out, "No! That's our doll!"

I looked at Shelly. Her eyes still held their excited gleam while mine were filling with tears. Now she wouldn't share it. If only Daddy hadn't said that it was Shelly's doll! Santa must have known the doll was for us both. Daddy had messed it all up. I wanted to tell Shelly how unfair it was. I glanced away from the precious doll in time to see Santa bringing another Matilda doll out of his sack.

I heard Daddy say, "I guess that one's Clair's."

Mine! All mine and she was even more lovely than Shelly's.

Whatever else Santa took out of that sack I didn't notice. Not even when he filled the stockings. My eyes were fixed on my Matilda.

Santa took a few more cookies and told Daddy he wished Mrs. Santa had the recipe. "She could keep me good and plump with these." He laughed. "Of all the places I've been tonight these are, with out a doubt, the best I've tasted."

"You haven't had too much trouble tonight I hope."

"Oh no. Not much. Things are going pretty fast this year because I didn't have to stop in Germany or Japan nor in some of those other countries. But that's good because without my elves I would have had way too much to do. Hitler doesn't even deserve a piece of coal in his stocking. But as I flew over I did drop some things for the children and our soldier boys."

Daddy shook Santa's hand and thanked him for coming to our house. We heard the sleigh scraping off into the night. We all burst into the living room as Daddy looked at us in surprise. "Y'all didn't go to sleep?"

Zeke hollered out. "No. We saw everything!"

We all started talking at once. I grabbed my dearest baby and held her close. She felt so cuddly and looked so sweet. I wrapped her in my sweater and warmed her. I smelled the newness of her and thought about how we'd stood in the store holding one and wanting one but never dreaming we could have one for each of us.

Christmas was a time for being free and playing instead of working.

It was a magical time. Just knowing there was somebody like Santa Claus who cared to come to our house and bring us toys was a wondrous feeling. There were sock monkeys, clothespin soldiers, yoyos, spinning tops, candy, oranges, nuts and apples. So many treasures from that land of magical splendor that we didn't know what to taste of first or play with next. Our fondest dreams had exploded over the room and the reality of it was magnificent. We had never had a Christmas this big.

Mother tried on a new Christmas apron that was hidden inside the branches of the decorated tree. She shoved her hands inside its deep pockets and twirled around. "I love it!" She danced. "I'll wear it into a pure rag."

Daddy had five cans of Prince Albert tobacco that he stood on the decorated mantel board. The red cans shone through the green boughs of cedar. Our bleak cabin had never looked, or smelled, so great. Christmas had filled the air and its decorations brightened the walls. This was the best Christmas ever, and our hearts sang.

Daddy and Mother took a box full of food and gifts for the cabin families. We wrapped up and drove to each house where Daddy placed a gift box on the porch and drove away laughing.

"You sound like Santa," Mother said. "Maybe this is why he's always doing that 'ho, ho, ho' sound." Her voice was full of joy.

We went to bed that night feeling warm and special with toys in our arms and Mother telling us about Jesus' birth and God's love for mankind. "It's always much better to give things than to get them," she said, "so always remember to give all you can, in all things and in all ways." She smoothed our hands open. "Only the opened hand can give as well as receive."

We drifted into a warm, sweet sleep.

Chapter Ten

March Wind

MARCH winds blew, war raged and Daddy ranted. By 1943, the stark reality of insurmountable bills hit him harder and harder every day. He fought to keep his head above water while losing more and more. He'd stomp around the house like some old pent up bull, hunting along the pasture for a downed fence post, fussing about being caught like a rabbit in a snare. "I'm not a man. I'm a slave. He's got me where he wants me. I can't get ahead and we're totally dependent on him. Roberts is a sneaky tyrant."

"We made the bills and we're the ones responsible for our situation. You know the Word says to owe no man anything but love," Mother said.

"You really don't need to be quoting Scripture to me right now. I'm ticked off. Roberts knew I wasn't thinking of anything like this when I ran up those bills. I still believe this war will end the world, but what I can't understand is Roberts acting like he does. Seems like he couldn't wait to give me a helping hand. Now I know it was to catch me here. He knew we were about to succeed. He knew it. I've seen him do the same thing to others. He suckers them in then extends credit…'if you'll just come in and sharecrop it out', yet when it's just about made where you can pay him and have some left over he lowers the boom. He's raised the payment again. That's unworthy tactics. I can't even afford tobacco. He's underhanded and that's wrong. You can't convince me it's right."

"I'm not trying to convince you of a thing. This is not his fault. How can it be? You're the one who borrowed and ran up that bill. Now you hate him because we made the choice to get into this kind of a mess. Nobody forced us. We're the ones who are supposed to plan like forever, but live as if it's our last day. We chomped off more than we could chew."

"He shouldn't have let me get in so deep that I couldn't pull myself out. I've been caught. It is a trap, you know. He's the one who knows what he's doing. Have you noticed folks acting like zombies? All their hopes and dreams for the future lost in the struggle to get a bite to eat and a place to lay their heads down. Every day that passes I'm becoming more and more like one of them."

As I listened to him talking I knew why I had felt an eerie feeling, like entering a graveyard, when we'd first come here. The life had gone from most of these people. They just existed and their songs were mournful wailings. There were no joyful sounds now, except for the Saturday night hoedowns, which were less frequent because folks would rather gather around the battery radio to hear the latest war news.

"Why don't you do the best you can?" Mother said. "Nobody can expect more than that. We'll get out of this. We need to think of our country and its problems right now."

Mother laid her hand on his shoulder and for the first time I saw Daddy push it away. My eyes filled with tears as he stomped out the door and slammed it behind him.

Mother quickly turned toward me and Shelly. "Why don't y'all run to the store and get me a small sack of sugar and I'll make a delicious dessert for supper." She pushed the money and a ration book into Shelly's hand then started stirring a pot of peas boiling on the stove. I threw my arms around her and hugged her. "Clair! What's gotten into you? You bounded into me like a wild Indian nearly knocking me into the pot."

"I love you, Mother. Forever and always."

"I love you too, Clair." She smiled at me.

As we were walking toward the door Zeke and Bay came bounding in. Zeke had a whirly-button caught tightly in his hair. He yelled at Bay who was continually saying, "I'm sorry, I'm sorry. It was an accident."

"What happened?" Mother asked as she wiped her hands on her apron and came over to Zeke.

"I gave Bay my button on a string for his penny and when he got it going like a circle saw he laid it over my head. He did it on purpose."

"You know I didn't mean to," Bay said. "I was just seeing if it would blow your hair and it got caught."

"Well, did you find out?" Mother said as she sent Shelly to bring the scissors. "I think you two boys hunt ways to get in trouble." She shook her head as she fumbled through the tangled mass of hair and string. As Shelly searched through the machine drawers I suddenly remembered that Mother had put them on the mantel board. I jumped up to get them and caught my dress over the dasher of the churn that sat on the hearth and pulled it over. Milk went sloshing over the floor like a white flood.

"Uh-oh." I stared at the mess. "But I found the scissors for you." I held them up.

Mother sat down, put her hands in her lap, then looked from me to Zeke to the milk to the ceiling. Shelly ran in and asked, "What happened?"

"I knocked over the milk churn while I was getting the scissors from the mantel."

"So that's where they were," Shelly said. "I have looked through every one of those blasted machine drawers."

While I was wiping up the milk Mother began cutting the toy loose from Zeke's thick hair. "Clair, when you've finished there, go see if you can find an egg or two for the cornbread."

I walked out the back door. I edged along the fence-line looking underneath the stemy grass of the broom sage field. There I spotted two fresh-laid eggs in the old blue-speckled ginny hen's nest. I gathered them and walked toward the door. I could hear Mother telling Zeke to take the coal oil can to the store with us. "I hardly had enough to wet down the kindling," she said. "I'm out of lighter knots too. See if you can pick up a few."

Bay was yelling about his penny because the button toy was ruined and he wanted to spend the coin at the store. Zeke said he was an Indian giver and Shelly said it didn't matter who spent the penny because the candy would have to be shared anyway. Mother threatened to take it away if an agreement wasn't made.

I walked in with the eggs and handed them to her. "I'm sorry I turned the milk over. I wanted to help but I made a mess."

Shelly was washing the cloth out in a dishpan of water. She looked up with her lips pursed. "I was the one who was supposed to get the scissors anyway. You could have told me where they were."

"Just like you've never done a thing wrong, Mrs. Prissy."

"Both of you calm down and go to the store before it gets too late. Zeke and Bay are going too. I need some coal oil. While you're walking think about how we should treat each other."

"Look at Zeke. His cowlick is gone. Now he'll have nothing to twist," I said.

"I'll just twist the front." He laughed as he curled his hair around his finger.

As we walked toward the store Maxine caught up to us and held out a tube of lipstick.

"Look what I found on the road but Momma won't let me wear it." She was out of breath.

"I can, I can." Shelly sang out as she took the bright red lip rouge and smeared it over her lips. It looked like it covered her face from ear to ear. The bright apple red glistened in the sunlight.

"Mama would skin me alive if I'd put that on my face." Maxine shook her head. "She says that kind of stuff is for old women and jezebels. Girls who paint up their faces is jezebels Mama said."

"Mrs. Neal don't wear lip rouge but Mrs. Effie said she was a jezebel," Zeke said.

"Do I look like one?" Shelly mashed her lips together and made a smacking noise.

"Maybe you do. I don't rightly know." Maxine shrugged her shoulders.

"We have an aunt who wears lip rouge and when she drinks coffee it stays on the cup. Once we wiped some of it onto our lips. When she kisses us she leaves lip prints on our cheeks." Shelly kissed the back of her hand. "Like this." She held it up.

Maxine laughed and smeared on some of the stuff and I did too as we kissed the backs of our hands to see our lip prints.

Bay, who was hunting for flint rocks, yelled. "I saw a thousand-legged worm. It's on that tall grass over there." He pointed.

"Are you sure it was a thousand legs?" We were afraid of them because if it counted your teeth you could die before sunrise unless you did the spell-breaker. So to be on the safe side, every time we saw one, we performed the ritual. It could have counted our teeth before we saw it. We all lined up and did the routine.

"Step back, spit in your track, turn around, count down, ten to one, charm's done."

As we walked along Zeke said, "If I ever passed a worm without seeing it and it counted my teeth, would I die and go to Heaven? And how do we get to Heaven anyway?"

I looked up and saw a crow flying over the cornfield loudly cawing, "caw, caw, caw." and I said, "Well, when we die we flap our arms like this and yell 'God, God, God', and he opens the gates for us to fly in."

Zeke smiled as we went hopping down the road flapping our arms and yelling "God, God, God". Yes, that would work if we were dead. Like that old black crow we'd fly away. And as the hymn says, "I'll Fly Away Oh Glory, I'll Fly Away." That's exactly how we'd get to Heaven.

When we got to the store Mr. Grey stared at us and frowned. "What's that on your faces? Looks like your lips are bleeding. Did y'all fall down and skin your mouths?"

"They put lip rough on themselves," Zeke and Bay said. "Maxine found it and they put it on their faces."

"Now why would such pretty girls want to go and mess themselves up for? At least they were pretty. Now they've messed themselves up good and proper."

"We're not messed up. It'll come right off."

We wiped at our lips and cleaned them. We looked under the candy counter where the best candies were laid on the shelves behind the glass. All we could afford was peppermint or licorice sticks. We could get more for our money if we got the licorice so that's what we did. Then Mr. Grey poured the coal oil in the can.

"Where's the nozzle cover?" He looked around.

"We never brought it. It's lost."

"I lose more potatoes this way." Mr. Grey fumbled through a bin of Irish potatoes and pulled out the tiniest one then shoved it down on the can's spout.

"There, now you won't spill it on the way. I'm sorry I can't sell you the sugar because you don't have enough points for it this time." He made the change. "But tell your Mother they're giving out sugar rations at the schoolhouse in the next couple days. Until then I'm sending her a cup of Mrs. Grey's. She can pay it back later."

We walked homeward and passed Mary Lou Clay. Shelly showed her the lip rouge.

"I wore this to the store," she proudly boasted.

"Oh, let me have some." She grabbed at the tube.

"You can have the whole thing if you'll jump the creek."

"I will. I've always wanted my own tube."

We walked to the creek. She leapt out and fell into the cold murky water. Then ran up the bank with her hand out.

"Give me the lipstick." She shivered in the cool air.

"No, it's not yours yet. I didn't tell you to jump in the creek I told you to jump across it. You didn't jump the creek. You fell in. You've got to jump all the way across it."

"I really do hate y'all. You know that? You're all idiots!"

"If we're the idiots how come you're the one standing here all wet and shivering, huh?"

"I'm telling on y'all!" She turned and stomped toward her house.

"Here, here, we're sorry. You can have the lip rouge!"

She turned, came back and snatched the tube.

"We were just playing with you. We were going to let you have it all the time. We're sorry you fell in. I don't know how come we did such a thing."

"I know why. Because you're all hate-filled and mean half-breeds and pick-a-ninnies!"

Zeke's back stiffened and with his eyes squinted he said to Mary Lou, "Hush up pig girl! Oink, oink." He snorted.

She went into a crying fit as she ran toward her house yelling, "I'm gonna tell my Mama on you!"

"Go on and tell her. She's at the trough! Oink, oink!"

I couldn't believe Zeke said that again after we had got the whey beat out of us for doing that before. We all knew that this was a sore spot with her. Last year when Mrs. Neal took us all over to Ned's house to watch a hog butchering going on in his backyard, Mary Lou said that she wanted the hog's lungs after Mrs. Neal had pointed out the hog's insides and jabbed at them with her long instructor's stick and said, "The lungs are like balloons. They can be blown up and deflated over and over again. This thin-looking skin is really tough."

So Mary Lou had hopped around squealing, "Can I have them? I want them, let me have them!" Until she got them.

After that day we laughed and told her that she had hog's lungs. We'd oink and she'd go into a squealing fit then we'd say, "See, don't that sound just like a hog squealing?" But we had quit picking on her about it until today because of the whippings we'd got.

Now Zeke had popped out with it again.

"Zeke, you're gonna be in so much trouble," I said. "You said it. We didn't."

"Well, Shelly started it with that darn lip crud."

"It was just a joke. I didn't think she'd really try jumping the creek for it."

"You know you can't joke with her."

When we got home Mother scooped out a stingy bit of sugar and stirred it in a flour batter that she fried into hoecake surprises. She'd top them with butter and honey for a delicious, sweet dessert or she would sometimes fold the cake over apples, peaches, jelly, cocoa or peanut butter, then crimp it together with a fork around the edges. We never knew what might be inside. That's why they were called 'hoecake surprises'.

After supper Daddy turned on the battery radio and we listened to the raving voice of Adolph Hitler declaring that he would destroy everyone against him or people who didn't do their fair share in his warring campaign. Then heard Winston Churchill telling about how well our boys were doing, yet the draft had been lowered to eighteen. So many of our boys were missing, others coming home dead or wounded.

The last time we'd gone to see the train the evening had turned cold and rainy. We sheltered ourselves under the porch of the depot and had noticed the groups of somber folks standing huddled and red-eyed. A loud burst of thunder shook the ground. The rains poured and beat down on the tin roof. It fell over the sides like a rushing waterfall.

"Even the angels are crying," Shelly had said.

The mourners waited for the fallen men coming home in pine boxes covered with the red, white and blue of the American flag. Even more unbearable than going to claim the draped boxes of brave loved ones was having nothing to claim. A son, brother, husband or Daddy was gone and the relatives never knew what had happened...never a proper way to say goodbye. People killing people wasn't natural yet the whole world was at war.

All our beliefs. All our ideals. All our understanding about everyone's basic conscience died in the face of worldwide destruction. The enemies grew more vulgar and evil as we saw tragic outcomes and the deep sorrow they instilled.

A lingering gray cloud hung over the train as it slowly rumbled away that day. The rains slacked off where we were. The morning angels had gone with the train to cry with others down the track. We no longer ran to see the train because it brought with it death, turmoil, grief and terror.

Tonight there was a bit of a chill in the air but the weather was getting warmer. As I lay in bed with Shelly, Zeke and Bay under the warm covers I wished for the music of Daddy's fiddle to softly sing me to sleep but it never came. Daddy didn't play much anymore. We all missed it.

Our school had a play about the upcoming spring and all parents were invited. It would take our minds away from the sorrow of war and poverty even if only for one night. The auditorium was packed full.

I saw Mother, Daddy and Bay and whispered to Shelly as I pointed. "There they are on the third row."

We peeped over the crocker sack ground where we, as flowers, waited to bloom. Mary Lou waited with her wand to tap the ground where we crouched. We waited to rise at her touch. Mrs. Neal tapped the floor and shushed us. Soon the play began. Farmer Bill hoed the ground and threw confetti seeds over our sack ground. We held it up in front of us. Peter Rabbit hopped over the stage looking for a carrot or something to eat. I popped up from the ground with my yellow crepe paper cap and scared him.

"What are you doing?" he asked. "It's not time for you to bloom."

"Oh Peter, when will it be time? We're so tired of waiting."

"I don't know. Let me ask Mr. Sun." Zeke with a big round cardboard sun in front of him moved onto the stage. "Mr. Sun are you going to come and warm the ground so the flowers can stay above the earth without freezing?"

"It won't be much longer. The flowers must wait until I get bigger and closer and warmer. Then I will send Mother Nature to touch their heads with her wand."

"See," Peter Rabbit said to me. "You must rest and wait until Mr. Sun comes closer and Mother Nature taps you."

"Oh dear, oh dear." Different flowers popped up and wilted back into the ground. "We must wait for Mr. Sun and Mother Nature."

"Yes," said Peter Rabbit, "then you will be warm and happy and you will not freeze when you come out of the ground."

The sun moved closer and walked the length of the stage. As he walked past, Mother Nature followed, tapping each of us on the head and we popped up dropping the crocker sack ground and we swayed and turned. We began to dance making two circles...purple violets in the center and yellow daffodils on the outside. Then we began to sing. The violets sang and danced clockwise while daffodils sang and danced counter clockwise.

We daffodils sang, "Daffodils, daffodils gaily go, gaily go, all in a circle, all in a circle, gaily go, gaily go."

The violets sang the same song except they said "violets" instead of "daffodils".

Then the curtain closed.

After the program I asked Shelly if she had gotten hit on the head as hard as I did by Mother Nature's wand.

"I noticed that she had to fix her little star back on the end when she got through tapping me and you. I almost bloomed all over her."

"Yeah. You can tell she's still mad at us."

When we got home we packed our costumes in the keepsake trunk. I wanted to keep the bright yellow socks out so I could wear them but they were also packed away.

When planting season came Daddy planted pickles on our plot of ground for a cash crop. He told Mr. Harris, the tallyman, "I heard a tale that pickles are going to sell like hotcakes this year and there isn't much to taking care of them."

"Just keep the vines on the rows so you can get in there to pick them. I'm telling you pickles grow like all get out! How much you figure on planting?" Mr. Harris said.

"I'm going to plant the whole plot in them. I really need the money."

"Just so long as you don't go knocking folks in the head to get it." He laughed as he rubbed his head. "That Jack Hicks hit me over the head and made off with all the cotton- picking money."

"Yeah, I heard about that. They're getting more brazen with their mess."

"I'm just glad Sheriff Springer caught the bastard! Looks like both those boys are going to spend their lives behind bars. I just know the rest of them Hicks children are coming right in behind them."

"I know what 'bastard' means," Zeke whispered to me.

"It's a dirty word," I said. "And you ought not be saying it."

"Yeah, but I know what it means. It's when a woman has a baby without a Daddy. She has the baby all by herself."

"Zeke. All babies have to have a Mama and a Daddy."

"Not bastards," he said.

"Who told you?"

"I heard Daddy and Mr. Hanks talking about this cousin of his that had a baby without a husband and that she kept it hid from everyone until she got married and told everyone that the baby was his. From then on it wasn't a bastard anymore."

"What if our Daddy dies or something?"

"Then I guess we'd become bastards."

"I thought you became an orphan."

"No, that's only if both your folks die. But if only your Daddy dies you become a bastard."

"What do you become if only your Mother dies?"

"I don't know. I guess that would make us the other dirty word. You know, bitches," Zeke whispered.

"I sure hope we are never 'bitches' or 'bastards'," I whispered back.

"What are you two whispering about?" Daddy looked at us.

"Nothing." We both said as we stood there with our eyes wide and bodies stiff as pokers as we desperately hoped he hadn't head what we'd been talking about.

"You two best get back to work now, the pickles aren't going to plant themselves."

Zeke took his place behind the plow as I guided Dolly.

We heard a car coming and looked up to see Mr. Roberts' gray Hudson. He drove over to where Daddy was sharpening the hoes. "What brings you out here?" Daddy said without looking up from his chore. "Got another increase on my payments to tell me about?"

"Not this week," Mr. Roberts laughed. "Don't be mad at me, Brown, you made the bill I didn't. Anyway, I'm going around telling everyone of you who has a dog to keep it on your own place. Some dog is killing my chickens and sucking the eggs too."

"Well, I don't know what dog it is, but I can tell you it isn't our dog."

"I don't care whose dog it is, just keep your dog on your own place. That's all I'm asking." He left.

Not long after this, dogs started turning up dead from eating glass or poisoning. One day we found Blacky lying on the ground groaning and bleeding at the mouth. We all started crying and huddled around him. Daddy came out to see what the fuss was about. He rubbed his finger in Blacky's mouth and came out with glass slivers.

"Kids, get in the house." Daddy went inside, loaded his gun and started out the door.

"No, Daddy don't," I yelled. "Don't kill sweet Blacky!"

"Clair, the longer we wait the longer Blacky's going to suffer. He's going to die because he's been hurt too bad. We can either be selfish and let him lie there and suffer till he dies or we can help sweet Blacky go on to where there's no pain."

"Okay, Daddy," I said with a sad heart.

We all hugged each other. Then we cried when we heard the gunshot.

Zeke got mad. "I wish I knew what coward did it!

"Shush now, come here." Mother hugged us all close. "It's okay, it's okay. Blacky's in a better place."

That evening we buried Blacky under the shade of the big chinaberry tree. We all stood around and said something nice about Blacky. It was hard to get used to not having him around when we would go fishing and not having him there at night to protect us. We would always miss him.

"If they only knew what a good ol' dog they'd killed, they'd be so sorry," Zeke said as he stood a cross up on the grave.

Chapter Eleven

Homecoming

PICKLES were everywhere. The more we picked the more they grew. As with most "hot tips" there was no demand for the blasted things. We ate pickles just about every way possible. Sweet pickles, sour pickles, bread and butter pickles, cucumber salad, fried cucumbers, baked cucumbers and even cucumber pie. Needless to say, we and all those around us, quickly got tired of them. Daddy swore that as long as there was breath in his body he would never plant another pickle.

The days were growing hotter. It hadn't rained in so long that the creek was just a narrow stream and the countryside lay covered in a thick layer of dust. Old folks sat outside under the shade trees fanning themselves. Most everyone else spent time at the swimming hole. We walked along the sun-dried dirt road. We waded the creek to the swimming hole to swim with the fish, otters, beavers and snakes.

Zeke whistled to the mocking bird and copied the bobwhite and the whippoorwill songs. Then he cupped his hands and blew between his thumbs to make a whistling sound. I had tried to 'blow my fist' but the wind blew right on through making a hollow sound.

The swimming hole was too shallow to use the rope swing but we could still slide down the bank and splash into the water. Floyd was there but he wouldn't bother me. We had come to an understanding awhile back. In our truce he would not pester me if I promised to be his girl when we grew up. I agreed. I was willing to promise anything to get him away from me right now.

Besides, who's to say what would happen before I grew up.

Daddy kept talking about the world ending. I hoped it would end before we grew up because I would never, ever, ever, ever like Floyd. Zeke and Floyd played and swam together. Me, Shelly and Bay were playing on the muddy slide that the otters had made by slithering in and out of the water.

Maxine and Mary Lou splashed at the sandy side of the water. They had an old bucket with nail holes in the bottom to catch the little minnows. They'd let all the water strain out then watch the little fishes flop and jump before they'd put them back in the water and catch others. Suddenly they yelled out. "A monster! We've caught a baby monster!" We all rushed over to see what it was.

"Look at it! Its got feet and everything!" I said.

"That looks like a lizard." Floyd told them.

"Lizards don't live in water...sea monsters do. That's a baby sea monster! Look on its head. Its like a dragon monster." Maxine pointed out.

"I know what that is. Its a salamander. I saw one in our science book. Its not a baby monster. That's as big as its going to get." Shelly said.

"I want it," Bay said, "can I keep it?"

"That thing is too scary for me, I don't want it." Mary Lou said.

"I certainly don't want that ugly thing. But I do want our bucket," Maxine said, "do you have anything to put it in?"

"I'll run home and get a fruit jar. I want it too." Zeke took off.

The boys went back to play as us girls sat with the strange looking creature.

"Did I tell you that I got a note from James yesterday? It was in with Mama's letter. He say for me to be sure and tell y'all 'howdy do' from him. He say for me not to let Momma worry about him and that ain't in no heavy fighting yet but he can't wait till he is. He thinks he could end the war all by himself if they'd just let him go fight."

"Our Uncle Hank is in New Guinea. He's on the USS Henley now. We got a letter from him too. He said nothing exciting ever happens on that big ol' ship. It's always boring and he misses us something fierce," I said.

"When he came home on a leave he brought pictures. He was with those New Guinea folks and dressed in their grass skirts and head garb. He even had his face painted just like them," Shelly said.

"We still don't know where James is." James hadn't been home even once since he left. "I sure do miss him."

Zeke came back with the jar and we dumped the thing in there with some water then he put the lid on it and handed it to Bay.

We went back to playing. I slid down the bank on my stomach and splashed in the water.

"I think I'll try that." Maxine ran up the bank.

While we were taking turns sliding down the bank another commotion caught our attention. We hurried toward the noise. Floyd was holding Toby the tar boy down while Zeke was doing something to his leg. "Be still you idiot!" Zeke screamed.

"No! Stop it! Stop!" Toby yelled to the top of his lunges while trying to break away from Floyd's grip.

Zeke had his rusty pocketknife opened and fixing to cut into his leg.

"What are y'all doing?" I screamed.

"Get off him!" Shelly demanded. "Leave him alone. Two on one ain't fair and Zeke of all things! Put that knife away right now!"

"He's been snake bit," Zeke said. "We're trying to save his life!"

"No! I'm not bit! I'm not bit! I was just joking! I scratched my leg on a berry bush. I thought it looked like a snakebite and decided to scare y'all! Let me up from here!"

"You don't do things like that," Zeke said as he stood and put his knife back in his pocket. "It's not funny and people could get hurt."

"Oh, shut up. I was the only one nearly got hurt. You with your rusty knife flipping out fixing to chop people's legs up and all."

After that, we decided we could go on home.

As we walked along the creek bank the sunlight flecked the beaten path as our bare feet sent dust puffs bursting behind our hills. A fluffy brown rabbit hurried into the bush to escape our hands. Thick gray moss swung from gnarled limbs that drooped from overhead. Mosquitoes as big as dragonflies buzzed in the deep shadows so we hurried through to the sunlight. Zeke had found some flint rocks and was hitting them together to make sparks.

"I heard a tale that some man down near the coast found a flint rock as big as a boulder," Floyd said.

"There ain't no such thing," Zeke said.

"There is too. I saw his picture in the paper."

We came out at the gravel road and ran into Joe Blass heading toward his whisky still. He had an empty bottle in his hand and was singing as loud as his drunken lungs would go. "Open up them pearly gates Lord I'm coming home."

"Maybe he thinks that still is heaven," Shelly said. "Cause that's where he's heading."

"He probably don't even know what he's singing, he's so drunk," I said.

"Howdy do." Joe looked at us trying to focus his eyes. "Y'all see them golden stairs?" He pointed the white lightning bottle.

"Yes, sir. We see them," Zeke said.

"You're lying to me. You don't see no golden stairs."

"Sure we do." Bay smiled.

"Then lead me to them so I can climb up."

"They're right over there." Bay pointed as we hurried away.

We turned and looked back. The old drunk was standing in the middle of the road lifting one foot and then the other till he fell. He'd get up and start climbing again.

"I guess he'll stand there stepping all day or until he passes out." Shelly laughed.

"Maybe we should have pointed him off the road."

"He's okay. You just about can't hurt a drunk," said Zeke.

We passed by Mrs. Neal's. She was outside in her backyard tying bottles on her pear tree. When the pears grew down inside them she would sell them at the county fair.

All this time had passed since Brother Paul's big announcement in church yet they still weren't married. Folks just figured they couldn't take the criticism of Mrs. Effie Clay. But they still said they were going to be married.

Mable Lee, the voodoo woman, passed by on her way to the creek.

She had her fishing pole on her shoulder and was wearing a big-rimmed straw hat. It was tied under her round fat chin with a scarf so that it wouldn't blow off. She looked at us. "They biting good?"

"We've been swimming. We haven't tried them out today."

"Then maybe I'll have a chance to get a few."

We watched her blue print dress being swallowed by the trees and shadows as she walked toward the creek.

"Well, that speaks highly of our fishing skills." I felt proud.

When we got home Mother was in a happy dither because she had gotten a letter from Uncle Edward. When letters came from our uncles we all knew to sit quietly and wait for Mother to get through reading them. At first there were blacked out words or lines to keep any enemies from finding out what was going on or where they were. Every letter was censored and stamped. But when they came home on leave it was "Katy bar the door" as they spilled out with explicit details and horrible happenings.

We got the good news in this letter that he was coming home on leave for a week. He was trying to get uncle Hank to get a leave at the same time. They hadn't seen each other since they went off to war. Everyone was excited about getting them home at the same time. Maybe it could be done. If so, it would be better than Christmas. We would go to D'Lo for the big family get-together. Mother spent the next few days getting us ready for the trip. It would be a wonderful homecoming with everyone there.

Mother sang as she packed and we flitted about deciding what we would take along.

I was so excited to be going somewhere again. I'd sat in this one spot long enough. My wonderlusting blood was thirsty for adventure. Mr. Roberts came by the house in a wild fit of pure graciousness and offered Daddy some travel money.

"No, Roberts. I don't want to owe you anymore than I already do."

"I'm just saying take it along, just in case. If you don't need it bring it back. It wont count against you."

"No thank you." Daddy went about his work.

"Madge, that husband of yours is just about as stubborn as a mule! Here, you keep the money." He shoved it into Mother's hand.

"I can't," she protested, "Cooper would be hurt."

"He don't have to know."

"I don't keep anything from my husband. Besides if we did happen to need it, how would I explain it to him? Its best if you take that on home with you." She thrust it back into his hand.

"Well, y'all hurry on back. There's work to be done around here."

Daddy asked Mother why Mr. Roberts had talked to her so long.

"He was trying to get me to take the money."

"You didn't take it, did you?"

"Of course not. But you know, he was just trying to be nice. You're too proud sometimes for your own good. I think you're jealous of his success, aren't you?"

"Inheritance isn't success, Madge."

"Well, without inheritance or success or whatever you call it, poor folks wouldn't have a job. You need to learn to be happy that you have work and that our children aren't starving without a roof over their heads. We're lots better off than a lot of people in this world.

"Alright, I'll go take the money. But I'll add it to the bill."

It was before daylight when we left the next morning. We were leaving a few days early because we wanted to be there a few days before our uncles got home. Mother wanted to help Grandma and the aunts get the house ready. The old home place must be perfect for their visit because Uncle Edward had written, "I tell you what I want when this war is over. A clean dry bed and plenty of soap and water."

When we arrived at Grandma and Grandpa's the aunts were already there. We all flew into cleaning the house. The deepest cleaning went into the bedrooms. Even the walls were scrubbed with strong smelling lye soap. The beds were taken apart, springs swept and washed along with the rails and slats. Mattresses were aired and sunned. The rooms sparkled like new pennies and smelled of sunshine and soapsuds. The happiest time was when they got there and the saddest was when they were leaving.

Uncle Hank didn't have any leave time and couldn't come. In his letter he said he could only get a leave in a dire emergency but be sure to tell Edward that he missed him and wanted him to take care. Then he said, "Mama, I didn't know how much I loved you all but when this war is over I'm coming home to be the best son any mother ever had. I miss home so much and I want to be there so bad. If I could I would run away from here and fly home as quick as a wink. Don't ever let anything happen to y'all. If you do get sick let me know. I need to hear from y'all. I'm sorry I can't be home. I know you've killed the fatted calf and worked your fingers to the bone for our visits. I can just see y'all now, sitting around the table, laughing and talking and wishing your sailor boy was there. I wish I was there too. There's no where else on earth I'd rather be but we've got to stop this evil and we all have to do things that are hard. Tell everyone to write me and I send my love, your sailor boy, Hank."

Even though we were disappointed that they both wouldn't be home we were very happy to see Uncle Edward. Everyone stayed glued to him as he told about how the fighting was going…about paratroopers landing in trees and getting shot before they could get loose…about some breaking ankles or legs yet hopping, running and scattering like field mice to get under cover. He said the foxholes they dug were often muddy and dank because the rainwater didn't dry good before the next deluge came. He told about them having to throw grenades inside places where they knew women and children were because if they passed them the Germans would jump out and shoot them down.

"The hardest thing I ever did was throw a grenade in a place where I could hear babies crying. Those rotten cowards use babies and women for a shield. Oh Mama, this one boy couldn't bring himself to throw a grenade and they ran out on him and shot him so many times no one could even recognize him. It was to do or die. I can't hardly stand it over there. I'm telling you I just live from letter to letter. I need that connection with y'all. I lose myself in the lines and it's like I'm home when I read them. Please, I am asking each and every one of y'all to never forget to write me. You can tell me about anything. I don't care, even if it ain't about nothing but that old crossed beak chicken out there. When you write to me it brings me home."

One night we were all awakened by a series of terrifying yells. Uncle Edward was having a nightmare about the war. Everyone ran to his room where we found him crouched over between the bed and the wall. Daddy started over toward him. "It's okay man. You're home now. It's just a dream." Uncle Edward pounced on him yelling.

"Get down Jimmy! Get down! You're gonna get hit!" He looked over at us. "Oh my God! We're surrounded. There's Germans everywhere."

Grandpa yelled at him. "It's us! Your family! You're home now! Wake up son!" Uncle Edward looked at us.

"Wh-wh-what are y'all doing in here? Is something wrong?"

"You were having a nightmare."

"I'm sorry did I wake everyone?"

"Pretty much got the whole countryside up. You were trying to get somebody named Jimmy to get down inside a foxhole." Daddy said as he stood up.

"Jimmy got killed last week. He was just a boy. He got hit by a mortar shell before he could get to cover. We were in the same platoon and I was trying to get him to cover. He didn't even look eighteen, he was such a little fellow."

Grandma wiped her eyes. "Well you're my little fellow. I want you to take care of *my* little fellow."

"We're all fighting for each other and for our country. America will stand tall and freedom will ring for every man, woman and child on the planet. We are all making deposits toward that day when all the world will be safe and at peace."

It seemed as if he had just got here when he was leaving again and we waved goodbye. We tried hard not to cry but as soon as he was far enough out of sight the tears came. Mother and Grandma and the aunts held tight to each other. Only afterward they would ease their heartaches and sadness by reliving every minute of the visit and every word that had been spoken by him. How he ate. How he sipped his coffee. How he polished his shoes. How he picked up a domino and how he laid it down. How he slept and how he combed his hair. These were our heroes so every move they made became etched in our memories until the next visit.

On our way home Shelly and I talked about how well the visit went. "Daddy and Grandpa really got along good didn't they?"

"Yeah, it wasn't just being nice. They really seemed to like each other. I was glad."

"I was too."

Chapter Twelve

From the Delta to Tennessee

SATURDAY was a warm sunny day so we went to the trickling stream to catch a few crawdads and fish for a while. We sat in the tall grass, poking our toes in the water and watching the sun's rays sprinkling over the ripples. They shimmered like millions of dewdrops and I decided that this was probably where all the dewdrops went. I lay on my back watching the tree's leaves fluttering like a swarm of green birds against the slow moving clouds. I felt the cool wind on my face and watched it wave over the grass, light as a feather brush.

I asked, "What is in the wind to make it move? How does it move things unless it has something that we can't see like a spirit or a ghost? What if we found out that wind was really something like a whole herd of spirit horses and we could even see them and ride them?"

"Well, if that's true I'll catch the lead horse and ride it all the way to the North Pole and back again," Zeke said.

We heard someone coming. They were walking along the gravel road making slow dragging sounds over the rocks. I looked over the grass and saw Lilac Rose, the voodoo woman's daughter that James told us about. The one who said she would use her hexing powers to kill L.Z. and sure enough, he came up dead! It was odd to see her out of the house. Lilac Rose never came around these parts. She was mumbling to herself as she shuffled along. Her words sounded all jumbled.

"Maybe she's chanting something evil," I said. "Let's get out of here!" We all leapt up and took off toward home.

I heard Lilac Rose gasp. "Lord a mercy!"

We disappeared around the bend. We were out of breath when we got to the house.

Mother was churning the milk, her hand moving in a learned rhythmic motion as the dasher sloshed. The thick buttermilk sent tiny drops spurting through the churn top and into the air like bubbly, white pearls. "What in the world are y'all running from? It's too warm a day to be flitting around too much. Y'all better slow down before you curdle your blood."

We sat on the porch steps to catch our breath.

"But Mother, Lilac Rose came by and she was chanting up all sorts of evil so we ran as fast as we could to get away."

"You don't still believe that tale, do you? You know James was just telling a tall tale. Well, I guess y'all didn't catch that mud cat then did you?"

"I thought I had caught that old big one but my line was caught on a limb or something." Zeke said.

"Sometimes I think that sucker is smart enough to take the bait and wrap the line around a limb." Shelly laughed.

"Well, to be that big, he's had to be around a long time. That means he's good at surviving and smart, too. It's likely no one will ever catch him," Mother said.

Daddy came in from the fields and sat on the steps with us. He looked tired and solemn.

"Shelly, go get your Daddy a cool drink."

"Levi says they got word that James was in a hospital in California," Daddy said as he took off his hat and wiped the sweat from his brow. "He's been hurt. They don't know how bad yet. "

"But I thought he wasn't in the fighting."

"Maxine said he told her he wasn't." I said.

"Oh, my stars. I must go see Boo!" Mother said. She told Shelly and me to take over the churning.

When Mother got to Boo she was sitting at the kitchen table holding the letter. She handed it to Mother. "I want to go see my boy. He needs his Mama."

"He needs his Mama to be strong and to stay calm. You've got to think of him."

"He's all I can think about. Look here what they sent me." She held out her shaking hand. "A purple heart. I get this but I don't get my boy.

Where's my boy!" She sobbed.

"We have to pray Boo. We have to pray for all our boys. This horrible war has got to end and that tyrant be destroyed off the face of the earth forever. We can't let fear and dread smash our hopes and dreams. Your boy's all right, Boo, I know. He's alive. He's just wounded and now he's coming home. You thank God, Boo. Thank God he's in the hospital and not in a pine box. You will see him again soon. I know it. He will return to you. You will be able to hold him in your arms again. Everything's going to be fine. God told me so. I trust God."

Boo put her face on Mother's shoulder and cried.

"Thank you, Mrs. Madge. Thank you! You are an angel of the Lord on this earth."

When Mother got home Daddy was sitting still in his chair. "I'm tired, Madge. So tired of being stuck out in the middle of a cotton field. Today when Levi told me about James I made up my mind. I have to do something. I've heard about this place in Tennessee where we can live in government provided homes while I work at a plant making batteries and things that our boys need. This is something I can do to help in the war effort. We're going. I'll go mad if we have to sit here another day doing nothing but filling Roberts' pockets. The debt is bigger than I can ever hope to pay while I sit here. I can make good money, from what I understand, and send payments back. This is an opportunity to get out of debt and help our country too. I need this."

Mother took the news as she always took it. With a deep breath, a prayer and then got to work preparing us for what lay ahead.

Not long after we were saying goodbye to all our friends and boarding a Continental Trail Ways bus. I was so excited to be getting on this great big vehicle as Daddy chased after some sacrificial involvement against the war monster.

Boo, Levi, Maxine and even ol' Floyd had come to see us off.

"Clair, now that you're leaving how can you be my girl when we grow up? I kept up my end of the deal and now you're running off and I'll never see you again."

As I looked into his sad eyes my heart rejoiced. I hadn't thought about that. Now I was free from him and the deal. I was liking Tennessee more and more every minute. "Well, I didn't break the agreement. I have to go where my folks take me."

"Well, if that's the way of it, then here." Floyd grabbed my arms and kissed me on my cheek.

I yelled at him. "You dirty mean thing. I'm glad I'll never have to see you again!"

"Bye sweetheart." Floyd yelled back as he ran off down the road.

I'm sure gonna miss y'all," Maxine said. "Be sure and write me."

"You write us too. Let us know about James. I'll send you our new address as soon as I know it."

Boo hugged Mother while Daddy and Levi shook hands and clasped each other around the shoulder. Then we climbed aboard and waved goodbye from the windows.

There were people everywhere. I settled down in my seat with Shelly and Zeke. Mother, Daddy and Bay sat across the aisle from us. Above the bus windows were signs. One had a picture of a soldier. There was a caption above his head, "We'll Take Care Of The Rising Sun," below him said, "You Take Care Of Rising Prices." With a list of seven keys to victory. Another one said, "Buy War Bonds!" Then there was the one with the old man on it called Uncle Sam. He pointed his finger at everyone that passed. It read, "Uncle Sam Wants You!" In big bold letters.

The drive would be long but comfortable. We got to eat on the bus and there was plenty of room to stretch our legs. We were going so fast that we were passing other cars on the road. We were so high up we had to look down to see the cars. I watched the bus's shadow sweeping along the way. It reminded me of a big blackbird following beside us and going where we went. Maybe this was a sign that I would see a white Dove. Could that bird have itself hidden in the foothills of Tennessee? A new beginning always lent wings to my heart and sent my hopes soaring, as high as the Dove.

We swept through towns with buildings so tall that I was sure they could fall over on top of us. They seemed to sway against the sky. I wondered if people inside them could feel them swaying. There was one above the others that had a long pole on top that pointed up like a needle poking into the clouds. Horns honked, motors whined and people were walking beside the road. They didn't wave. They didn't talk. They didn't seem to know we were there watching them. There were buses whizzing by with tall poles hooked on wires. When they turned a corner fire and sparks shot out from their poles.

Daddy looked at us and said, "Looks like ants on a hot bed of rocks out there don't it?"

We all laughed. The bus stopped and we got off to get a snack. There were signs that said 'restaurant' and 'restroom'. I asked what they meant and Daddy said that we could eat there or use the toilet. I couldn't find a connection. Restroom and toilet didn't fit anymore than restaurant and food. So I supposed it was because you sit and rest at both places…resting to eat and resting to use the toilet. But I wasn't about to sit on that thing. Mother told me to pretend it was the slop jar at home. That was just fine until Mother pushed a handle down and made that big white slop jar thing start bubbling, gurgling and churning up the water inside. It was about the worst undercurrent I'd ever seen and it was probably strong enough to pull me down inside. I couldn't wait to get out of there.

As we neared our destination, I could see the mountains in the distance. The Great Smokey Mountains. They are a part of the Appalachian range that borders Tennessee and North Carolina. On the sides and valleys of these mountains was the war plant and town where we would live.

When we got there we were loaded onto an Army truck with a flap that fell across the back. It flapped in the wind like there was a violent storm outside. The ride was rough. Then we came to a checkpoint. They checked the badges on the driver and the men before they let us pass. We pulled to a stop in front of a row of houses all made alike. They were perched on the side of this tall mountain. The ground was bare. All these houses and roads had just been built. There hadn't been time for the grass to grow from where the mountain's forests had been cleared away. The land had been dug and turned and trampled to make way for this war plant and the people who would live and work here behind these gates. I was afraid to step out of the truck because everything was so different. I don't know what I expected but there were houses everywhere. There were small yards but no pastures or fields around them. The fronts of the houses were level with the ground and street in front of them where a red wooden box sat.

"What's that?" I pointed to the red box.

"It's a coal bin. These houses are heated with coal," Daddy said. "Aren't you going to get down out of the truck?"

We walked up to a house…a beautiful house. Daddy said that it was ours. Inside there were no lamps or candles, only small buttons on the walls that could be pushed and out of nowhere light streamed into the room. There was water that came through things called 'taps' or 'spigots' that you could turn and the water would spew out. We didn't have to draw it out of a well anymore. Anytime we wanted water all we had to do was turn that star-shaped knob and water would come gushing out. It felt like we'd rubbed some magical lamp.

"I bet you won't see rats coming through these little pipes, Madge." Daddy laughed.

We didn't even have to go to the outhouse anymore. There was a toilet right inside but I was afraid of that loud, gurgling, swishing, sucking hole. I thought if it pulled me down into it that I'd be lost and gone forever.

In the bedrooms the beds looked like crisp straight boxes, not fluffy and misshapen like the feather ones at home. I thought they looked hard and I said so. "It might feel like we're sleeping on a table."

I didn't like the look of it. Daddy picked me up and tossed me on it. I closed my eyes waiting for the impact. I just knew it was going to be as hard as the table. When I landed in the middle I bounced. It was soft and nice. I couldn't believe it. From the way it looked I didn't think it could have any softness at all.

There were little rooms in the bedrooms that Daddy said were closets.

"What's a closet?" I asked as I peered inside.

"That's where we hang our clothes," Daddy said.

"A whole room just for clothes? Who in the world has so many clothes that they'd need a room for them all?" Shelly wanted to know.

"We'll have tons of store bought clothes soon," Daddy said.

We all rushed out back to see what wonders awaited us. A small porch was there with rails around it and stairs leading to the ground. The back of the house was held up with large crossed beams. It scared us to see that our house dangled in mid-air off the side of a mountainous hill. There was a clothesline in the backyard and wooden sidewalks that separated each house. They were being added because of the mud. Straight down the mountain was another level of houses and streets. On that level was a store. Above us were still more houses. We heard music from inside so we ran back in.

Mother and Daddy were dancing around the living room.

"Aren't we going to waste the batteries in that radio?" Shelly asked.

"We have a radio that we can plug in. It won't ever need batteries," Daddy said.

"How can it do that?" I asked.

"It's called electricity!"

Daddy laughed as he went back and swung Mother around. Her shoe had torn loose from its sole clear back to the arch. When she'd step she'd flick the loose sole to make it flip straight under her foot so it wouldn't fold back in a curl and trip her.

Daddy sang, "Dancing with a dolly with a hole in her stocking."

Mother laughed and pushed him and told him it wasn't her stocking. It was her shoe.

The next day Daddy went to work and we began school. The schoolrooms were different than any we'd ever seen. There were no desks. There were long tables formed into a large square with chairs sitting around them. There was a box on legs that held what looked like dirt. I wondered why a classroom would have a large box of dirt in it.

It wasn't long before this dream world turned into one of the worst nightmares we'd ever had. There was a deeper fear that enveloped this secured little town with its fences and guards at its gates. This was a top secret city. People didn't go and come at will. Daddy had to wear his badge almost every where we went. Night sirens would abruptly screech out for a total 'blackout' and not even a cigarette could be lighted. It stretched out into the surrounding town of Knoxville. We were all stuck in that eerie darkness. When the sirens would sound my breathing would get caught in my throat until a scream came ripping from me. I was warning everyone that I was about to die. I needed help, air, light. I needed my world.

Mother came and held us close but I still felt far away. It was a distance that the darkness caused. I needed to see her face. If I could just see her smile I would know everything was all right. "Shush, Clair. You're scaring Bay. The lights will be on soon. Listen and I'll tell you all the story of Jack Rabbit."

As she told the story there was the loud roar of planes overhead like a fearful droning that could wipe us away in minutes. I knew the Japs had suicide bombers that could dive in and kill us all. The level of security here was as if we were sitting in Germany because their spies were coming into America. This place, hidden in the mountains, must remain a secret! In my little child's mind, something dreadful was going on here. We picked up on the adult's fear and knew if they were scared, we were not safe at all and it was terrifying. We'd come from a world of lanterns, wells and outhouses to one of electricity, gates, check points and night sirens. Bay was so scared that he stayed glued to Mother almost all the time.

Before another blackout came Mother took shades and quilts to make a darkroom where we could go and have a lantern on. Mother and Daddy would make hand puppets on the wall for us to watch. We had to whisper and quietly listen until the 'all clear' beeps sounded. The light and these quiet games stilled our fears.

Every day the radio played and filled the house with songs like "Wild Blue Yonder," "Field of Artillery," "Smoke on the Water," and "Philippino Baby." The newspapers were full of stories about the war and our brave boys and things to lift the people's spirits, but there were other stories about boys who'd been killed or wounded and stories about German spies infiltrating America. Some had been arrested. The papers called them the *Florida Four.*

We weren't safe. The world wasn't safe and we had never been more aware of it than now. Here in this place there was nothing but the danger of discovery and instant death. It seemed to me like the whole world was going to keep right on fighting and killing until nobody was left. I wanted to go back home to that time when there was no war and things were simple. I missed everyone and our life there. I even missed picking cotton. The times we'd spent in the fields with each other and our friends, inventing games and being carefree.

All I heard from Daddy was rations, war, Pearl Harbor, Roosevelt, government men, war plants and blackouts. I already knew that they meant some nights we could have a light and some nights we couldn't or that Mother couldn't go to the store without those rectangular stamps with pictures of guns, ships and planes on them and that we must pray every night for America and the end of the war.

Mother saved all her leftover grease and tin cans for the war effort. We saved ten-cent stamps in our war bonds books. One of Zeke's friends named Alexander had his picture in the paper for the kid with the most war bonds. He had twenty-five books. None of us could seem to get one book filled. We would sit around the radio listening to the war news. Roosevelt promised us victory and Churchill gave us his "victory" sign in the newspapers but no victory seemed to come.

It was the last day of September when we got word from Grandma and Grandpa that Uncle Hank's ship, the USS Henley, had been hit by a torpedo. He was all right they said. Only about fifteen had been killed. Mother broke down crying. This increased her fears about how vulnerable we all were. That maybe the next ship sunk would get Uncle Hank. The next grenade would get Uncle Edward or the next German spy or suicide bomber would get us. One US war plant had already been blown up. A ship off the coast of New Jersey had been hit. The SS Gulfamerica sank off the coast of Jacksonville after it was hit by a torpedo from the German U-Boat, U-123. It could be seen by the people on the Jacksonville Beach. Debris and the dead washed onto our US shores. The German attack against the US east coast was called, *Operation Drumbeat.* We had lost 238 ships in the first 9 months of 1942 alone.

The war demon was inching in on us more and more every day and our greatest fear was that we could not stop him. Even if we finally did stop him how many of us would be left? There was not a family here that didn't have at least one member fighting overseas to keep the homeland free. So all of America worked hard day and night to pump energy, hope, supplies, letters and prayers out to their brave loved ones.

This unity held America together but there wasn't a minute, at least not in this place, that we could truly believe that we were safe. Anything could happen at anytime. The threat was real. The seething monster was banging at America's door and we heard him loud and clear. There was not a minute that we could let down our fight to keep the door tightly barricaded. We gave our blood. Our tears. Our sweat. Our prayers. Children happily gave tooth fairy or any money they got for a ten-cent war stamp to put in their war bonds books. We had never known anything like this in our lives and hoped we never would again.

Time dragged by in cold icy days and wind-howling nights while the war raged. It was sweeping us up in a fear creeping like a wild vine over the entire countryside. We didn't ask for this but we had to keep fighting and supporting our boys. We had to pray and we had to keep hope alive in the face of everything.

Every so often men in coveralls would come around the house with beeping machines and with wands in their hands. They were listening for some loud beeps or something. We didn't understand what it was all about. It was foreign and alien here. Things were so different. Nothing was just normal. We were locked away from everything we had ever known before. This certainly was a frightful and strange place with its electric lights, running water and sloshing slop jars. This was a place of secrets to stay until the world could be safe from war…until Hitler and the Japs were destroyed. We lived in these communities of schools, supermarkets, churches, movie theaters and shopping centers. We built warm, loving relationships with others who were also locked behind these secret and censored gates…a community of houses so close together that only a board sidewalk separated them.

There were all kinds of *riff-raff*, as Mother called them, scattered within these neighborhoods. Sometimes the police would find dead bodies here and there and never knew who did it. One day we were going down to the next level through the path to the store when a strange man grabbed me and pulled me into the bushes.

Shelly, Zeke and Bay took off screaming.

Mother, who was watching from the porch, started yelling and running with her broom in hand. All the women heard her and grabbed their brooms, frying pans or anything they could hit with and followed her.

He heard them coming and took off.

They all ran past me and caught up to him. They beat him down the hill to where a policeman saw the commotion and took over. He put him in handcuffs and threw him, battered and bloody, into the back of the car.

All the women stood there fixing their falling hair, still clutching their brooms and frying pans, while Mother held me close.

"Are you alright?" Mrs. Ruby asked me. "Did he hurt you?"

"I'm fine. But why did he want to look at my drawers?"

"I guess he wanted to see what color they were." Mother hugged me tighter and cried and laughed at the same time.

She took us all home and we never again got to leave the yard without her. I wondered how many other colors of underpants there were. All I'd ever seen were white.

Chapter Thirteen

Granny One

OUR neighbor had three children. There was a boy my and Zeke's age and twin girls Shelly's age. They were from Mississippi too but they talked like Yankees. It was hard to understand them sometimes. They said every morning that they had to take their chill tonic to keep them well. I supposed it was something like Mable Lee's conjured up potion to ward off the miseries. But Alexander said it was because he and his sisters had played with a boy down the way who'd come down with polio. When we told Mother about that we couldn't play with Alexander or his sisters until Mother was sure that they hadn't caught the polio from that boy.

We liked going to their house because of their Granny. We all called her Granny One. She was about the best entertainer in the whole world. She'd make spool toys, hand puppets and other such things that children find amusing. We liked her stories best of all.

The twins' names were Judy and Julia. These two girls were as opposite as night and day. Zeke and I liked Judy the best because she read Superman comics like we did and we could exchange books and talk about them. Judy was like a wild ride on a roller coaster. She was a thinker, an inventor, a doer of life. It was as if she were fighting the entire universe to bend it and shape it to fit her own idealistic world…the exciting and different world of Judy Dickinson. She was like a walking encyclopedia. No matter what the question was she had an answer. We liked her because she reminded us of ourselves. She was like a wave of the sea going against all the other waves…like a sunset at dawn and a sunrise at dusk. She soared like a kite rising on the wind, while Julia, practical Julia, held the string on a steady course.

Julia was disciplined, cautious and stable. She was noble, kind, levelheaded…looking not only once, but twice or more, before she'd leap.

Julia could figure the cost of a whole list of things within a few pennies by adding them in her head. She could take command of any situation and was neat, punctual, quiet, faithful and steady. She existed in the shadow of Judy's happy-go-lucky nature. She and Shelly were best of friends. They stuck together like peanut butter and jelly. Where you saw one you saw the other.

Granny One was going to celebrate her ninety-second birthday that Saturday and we were all invited. For her birthday present her granddaughter had fixed up a photo album of Granny One's pictures. It was full of old tin plates. There was one of Granny One right after the Civil War when she was about fourteen. She was beautiful with her long dark hair and a crown of rosebuds holding it back. She wore a white flowing gown also trimmed with roses. She stood tall and slender with her graceful hand propped on the back of a chair.

"I was married the very next spring after this picture was taken," she told us. "Benjamin had been in the Civil War. I guess he was about five years older than me. He was so young when he went off to fight, fifteen, I believe. I can still see him when he left, hopeful and proud. I remember how much he had changed when he came back. He was beaten down and just about starved to death. I knew him all my life and I loved him from the start. The day he left Yazoo I felt like I was going to die right there on the spot. I was so angry that he had to go.

There was no call for that war. It was pure stupid. As stupid as the hot-headed bunch who caused it. There was nothing that couldn't have been settled over a cup of tea if everyone with an opinion about anything hadn't tried to force that opinion down the other's throat. I don't mean to rattle on about that. I just remember Benjamin was so dirty and sick when he got home everyone thought he was going to die. They said he wouldn't sleep because he was so scared of dreaming about what he had seen. At times he would drift off and wake up crying and shaking. I had to go take care of him. I would feed him and talk to him. He always wanted me to sing. He said it cleared his mind. Day after day I was there and while I sang he would sleep and rest as sound and peaceful as a new baby that had never seen or heard anything bad.

Soon he was well and as spry as ever. He started coming around to court me. Then we were married."

Julia pointed to a picture of a little girl about two years old. She had a chubby round face and curly blond hair in which a ribbon was tied in a big bow. "Who is this?"

"That's my little sister, Georgiana."

"Where is she now?"

"She died from the fever shortly after that picture was taken." The little girl's face looked like the face of one of the cherubs I'd seen on Christmas cards.

"Doesn't it ever bother you?"

"When she first died we all cried most all the time until one night I saw her in a dream. She was walking in a row of little children. They each had a brightly lit candle except Georgiana. I asked her why her candle wasn't lit too and she told me that our tears kept it put out. I never cried after that. I told Mama and Papa about the dream and they stopped crying too. Mama brought out all the things that she'd put away. Georgiana's pictures, books and toys. It was like seeing her again."

Granny One pointed to a picture of herself wearing a long black dress and high-button shoes. She looked little in this picture.

"This was about the size I was when I beat some Union soldiers out of our barn." She laughed. "Look at how little I was. I was a spitfire."

"What happened?" Zeke asked.

"Well, I reckon I was about twelve that summer. Yeah, I was. I had gone to the barn to do my milking like I did every morning. I heard a commotion outside and climbed in the hayloft to look out the opening. I saw a group of about four Yankee soldiers. They were robbing our chicken coop. They would grab a chicken, wring its neck and throw it in their sacks. Some were heading toward the house.

I yelled at them and said, "You get on away from here you lowdown Yankee thieves!"

They turned and headed toward the barn. I looked around for anything to protect myself with when my eyes landed upon a pitchfork. Just as the first Yankee's head was peeking above the loft floor I whacked him one good time and down he flew knocking off the others who were climbing up behind him. He lay on the ground a little while before getting back up. I thought I had killed him. Another tried coming up and I pushed the ladder away from the loft and he went sailing onto the ground. They killed our cow and set the barn on fire with me in it. They thought there was no way for me to get out cause I had pushed the ladder away. When they rode off I jumped out on a pile of hay under the hayloft opening and ran to the house. No one was there. Everyone had gone to the storm pit to hide while I was taking care of the Yankees in the barn."

Till night fell we were looking at pictures and hearing funny, sad, happy and exciting stories of Granny One's long life. Every picture she saw held another story and we were all ears. Her stories were so vivid I could see them. I saw her Papa returning from a trip with a present for her birthday. I saw her opening the music box and I heard it playing. I saw her Mama making her wedding dress with the cathedral lace that she wore. I saw her Papa walk her down the aisle. I saw her step into the black leather buggy and drive away sitting beside her new husband while she nervously twisted the gold band on her ring finger. I heard the katydids singing to the evening skies filled with starlight. I felt her excitement. I saw her growing older raising her family. I felt the joy as she held her first grandchild and the pain when she buried her loving husband.

"I almost had a conniption fit when I found out that Florence was going to marry a Yankee. But time has a way of making things heal. He's been a good father and husband too. Despite the fact that's he's a Yankee," Granny One said as she looked at a picture of her granddaughter's wedding day. "But you just have to let the past be the past, don't you?"

"That's right Granny One," Mr. Dickinson, the Yankee, said as he kissed Granny One on her cheek.

"I've had a rich and sweet life." She sighed as she closed the album. "I'm content. It does pain me that there are Hitlers out there bent on being as evil as they can. Seeking to do the devil's bidding and loving it. Loving to kill, steal and destroy. I have seen a lot of war in my day and here I am going through another one. We'll just hope for a brighter day, won't we?" She winked at me.

"We almost forgot the cake," Mrs. Dickinson said as she jumped to her feet.

She came back with a large chocolate cake. It had a straight row of nine candles and under that a row with just two to stand for ninety-two.

Granny One looked around before she blew them out and said, "You know. I don't have a thing to wish for. Why don't you kids come and make some wishes while we all blow them out together?"

All of us with our eyes closed wished as hard as we could for things we wanted and blew them out as a shrill blackout siren screeched. I didn't get my wish yet.

The next morning we went to church. All of us sat together on one pew. Judy brought her new Superman comic book. We looked through the pages before the service started.

"You should put that away." Julia said. ""Y'all shouldn't be reading it in church anyway!"

"It doesn't matter where we read it, if its okay to read outside of church its okay to read inside church." Judy told her.

"But this is a special time that we set aside for the word of the Lord. Not for Marvel Comics! You need to put it away."

"I'll put it away when Brother McGinnis gets here. Is that alright with you?"

"Its perfectly alright with me. I could care less, you're the one who's going to get in trouble."

"Mind your own business."

Just about that time we heard Mrs. Dickinson's voice behind us. "Stop fussing in church! You're both in trouble when we get home!" She snatched the book from Judy's hands. "Both of you sit up and behave yourselves."

Just then Brother McGinnis came in. He was a tall and slender man with a deep voice and crystal blue eyes that glittered when he was full of the spirit of the Lord. He radiated love. We'd all put down anything we were reading to hear him. None of us could miss a single church service without feeling we had missed something great. Especially me, Shelly, Judy and Julia. We all four had a crush on Brother McGinnis. He was a very handsome and sweet man. He would speak to the children as well as the adults and would even shake our hands as we were leaving. Everyone seemed to like him. But I was sure that no one liked him more than me.

The church was quiet as he walked straight to the podium and propped his hand on it. He looked at the congregation and began his sermon, "I've heard that some folks are trying to explain this war in human terms." His voice was strong and sure. "I've heard people asking why God would allow such a thing to happen. All I have to say to you about that is man is imperfect. God created us in his own image with a free will choice. All sin is a choice." He leaned forward, looking straight at the congregation. "Nobody forces us to sin or to go against what we know is right." Julia looked over at Judy and smirked as she nodded her head. Judy rolled her eyes and turned away.

"From the very beginning Satan whispered lies and rebellion in the garden and our first parents choose to disobey God so sin entered the perfect world. Hitler has chosen to disobey." He pointed into the congregation. "You know when you do wrong and so does Hitler. He and his allies are in direct rebellion against God and His people, therefore they will lose this war! Even if we had nothing but the jawbone of an ass, just as Sampson, we would defeat the enemy. Trust everything to the mighty Creator and don't lose faith. Rest in His love and protection. We are to keep our eyes on Jesus, not on fear. Concentrate on peace and victory. Speak to the harsh winds and tell them to be still!" His voice resonated through the church as the words he spoke filled my heart with hope and joy. I truly felt like I could speak to the winds and tell them to be still. I was lost in his powerful sermon as he continued. "We are God's family and because of that the devil hates us. He wars against us and seeks to take us over but good and evil will never mix.

Good and evil resides in each of us, but like oil and water, they will never mix. One will take over! If you take the oil out, the water flows into its space. Hittler has shoved anything good, Holy or righteous away from him. Hate and evil have taken him over completely and that is not God's fault.

"Remember that in our own lives its up to us to shove out the bad so that good will flow into its place."

The service ended with a hymn and a prayer. Brother McGinnis stood at the doorway shaking the hands of the congregation as they filed out of the church.

Mother said, "I really needed that sermon, Brother McGinnis. Ever since Hank's ship got hit I have been in dread and fear."

"It's in God's hands and not ours, Sister Brown. Keep the faith." He smiled.

When we got home Mother said Brother McGinnis was talking straight to her when he said that about fear and all. Then she said, "I think we need to have parties when the blackouts come." It was funny because I felt like he was talking directly to me too.

After this she would fix goodies and games that were only for blackouts. We would call them "blackout cookies", "blackout fudge", "blackout jacks" or "blackout rummy."

Shelly and Julia sat on the steps writing. They had taken to writing poems and were pretty good at it. When they would finish one they would gather everyone and recite it together. My favorite was the one titled "I See."

I see through the holes in Jesus' hands,
A happy ever after land,
I see in the stripes on Jesus' back,
Satan no longer can win the attack,
I see from the thorns on Jesus' head,
He is exactly what He said,
And I see when the stone was rolled away,
My Jesus will come for me someday.

That one was so good that they got to recite it in church. Everyone loved it. From then on they couldn't stop writing poems. They would sit together for hours jotting down lines then scratching them out and trying again till they got it exactly right. They wrote funny poems, sad poems and spiritual poems. The funniest one was the one Shelly wrote about our poor dead rooster.

I had an old pet rooster whose name was Uncle Sam,
One day me and sister baptized him till he drowned.
I wrote this epitaph and laid it on his grave,
Here lies my rooster Sam, who died when he was saved.

Julia tried a funny one on her own about Hitler.

Hitler and Satan sitting in a tree,
K-I-L-L-I-N-G.
First comes defeat
Then comes surrender
Here comes Hitler smashed by our defender.

Shelly and Julia walked to the Dickinson's to recite their latest poem to Granny One who was on their back porch rocking and tatting. We soon followed them over there and sat down. We watched Granny One as she slowly rocked her chair back and forth. Her gentle face was full of the wisdom and contentment of many years well spent. There was no regret, no cheated look about her and she tatted away as she rocked. The shuttle moved swiftly back and forth, up and down, between her fingers and through the thread as a lacy edging, tablecloth or whatever emerged longer, wider and lacier. The rhythmic creaking of the old rocker on the planks was a comforting sound. She stopped her work long enough to listen to them recite their poem and to make us loops of thread to put over our hands. Then she proceeded to show us how to make Jacob's ladder, cup and saucer, crow's foot and cat's cradle. We all sat there playing with the finger threads as she returned to her work.

Her hair was raked up into a cottony ball at the nape of her neck as loose wisps stroked the air like fine spider's webbing. Shelly admired her work "That's so pretty, I wish I could do it."

"She showed me how." Julia said. "I could help you learn."

"Sure, Julia knows all there is to know about all that kind of stuff. But I think its boring." Judy frowned.

"Me too," I said. "Its too puzzling for me to figure out."

"Its not boring, its fun learning how to do things that will help me become a good housekeeper someday."

"I don't have any use for all that. When I grow up, I'm going to be a doctor. I'm going to go with the Red Cross and help people all over the world."

"You mean a nurse, don't you? There ain't no girl doctors." Zeke informed her.

"Hold on there, young man. You're sitting here with a woman doctor at this very minute."

"You're a doctor?" We all looked at her in amazement.

"Sure am. I always had the knack from the time I'd nursed my Benjamin back to health. Back in my day, right after the civil war, when old Doc Gary was out rambling around in his buggy and seeing to folks, he use to come by my house and get me to go help him. I learned a lot about medicine and tending the sick for which I was beholding to him, not dreaming that one day I'd be the doctor myself.

"Yep, I reckon I was the first woman doctor. At least I was the first one in Yazoo Mississippi.

"One cold winter night the old Doctor died. Had worked himself to death out in that infernal cold weather. It was one of the coldest winters we'd had since the winter of 1845. I was born a few winters after that, so I'd never seen cold like this. Anyway, I had to take over Doc Gary's work until a new doctor could be found. I pretty well knew it would be spring, or later, before anyone came, so I had to be the doctor all by myself for a long while. No matter if I was a man or woman, they needed me. There was an outbreak of influenza that was sweeping through the entire town and showing no mercy. People were dyeing like flies. Entire families were being wiped out. I worked day and night trying to contain it. I don't mind telling you, I was scared. But afterward the people looked at me as their Doctor even though the new doctor did come. So you see, Zeke, ladies can be doctors."

"Well, maybe I'll be a nurse then." Zeke laughed.

"Don't laugh too hard, pretty well could happen."

The mail man passed so we got up and ran home. "See y'all later!" We said as we hurried down the steps.

There was a letter from Maxine. James was home she said, but he was not the same. His leg had been shot too bad to save. Nothing pleased him anymore. This man who once found pleasure in the smallest things was now a stranger. She didn't know how to talk to him or what to do. She had lost James unless she could find a way to bring him back.

"All we try to do is make him happy and he's never happy. Mama is at her wits' end and Pappy just ignores him. I don't know what he needs. All I know is he was never meant to go to war. It's ruined him."

Boo's letter to Mother said the same thing. Poor, sweet, forever strong Boo was beaten by this. She could withstand back-breaking work and poverty but she could not withstand her child hurting. It was all too much for her.

Mother laid down the letter and closed herself in her room. Behind that door we knew she was on her knees. We found a quiet place to do the same.

Chapter Fourteen

The First Snow

DADDY bought an old green truck that would, or wouldn't, crank depending on its whim. But we were excited about going to the store and riding in it. We just hoped it would go there and back. In this green leapfrog nothing was an absolute. It dictated whether or not we went anywhere. But then again, Daddy didn't know how to drive the thing. He would jump it down the road swerving from side to side before getting it going good. One day while we were going to the store he put the thing in the ditch.

Mother yelled, "You still can't drive this thing! This piece of metal is going to kill us all!"

"It was loose gravel. I can drive. It's been raining. I slipped off the slick pavement, hit some loose gravel and it caused me to wind up in the ditch."

"You hit a loose screw in your head Mr. want to be big driving a truck."

"Well, you liked the idea too Mrs. wanting to ride to and fro lady."

"Yeah, if I'd get to and fro and not pitch in the ditch! And you can't drive. You can't steer. You can't hardly even start the darn thing!"

Mother took us all and started walking home and left Daddy to get the green monster out of the ditch. It was cold out today and overcast. We were all bundled up well. As we walked I felt moisture hitting my face. I looked up to see thousands of little ice crystals swirling in a frenzy above my head.

"Look!" I pointed upward in excitement.

"It's snowing!" Zeke shouted.

"No, not snow. Only sleet," Mother said. "But it might be snow before too much longer."

By that evening the first snow of the year was drifting down from heaven like soft downy feathers. "Looks like the angels were fluffing God's pillow and busted it," I said.

"Maybe the angels are molting." Shelly laughed.

"Maybe y'all would like to have some snow ice cream," Mother said.

Outside in the new fallen snow tiny snowbirds danced and hopped over the smooth surface. Mother handed us cornbread. "Drop crumbs in a line, hold some and wait. The snowbirds will come." Mother took the dishpan and a spoon and scooped the top off the clean white snow. "For snow ice cream. It will be a delicious surprise when it's done."

We held out our hands with the crumbs for the snowbirds and when they came we squealed in glee. This was the very first time we'd ever witnessed birds that came up to us. They were even eating the breadcrumbs out of our hands.

Alexander, Judy and Julia ran over. The birds scattered. "Let's build a snow man." Judy said.

"No, let's feed the snow birds." We gave them some of our crumbs. The birds slowly came hopping back. After all the crumbs were gone, we all went inside and watched Mother make the snow ice cream. She beat milk, vanilla flavoring, sugar and eggs in a saucepan then cooked it before pouring it over the snow, stirring it quickly. We gorged ourselves on the sweet cool goodness as we listened to the "Blondie and Dagwood" show. It always started out with a yell, "Bloooondie!" After that they left and we helped Mother clean up the dishes.

When Daddy came home and parked the awful green thing, he came in with groceries and a slender, white box that he handed to Mother.

She opened it. "Nylons! It's a pair of nylons. You don't mean it!" She ran her hands over them gently. "I had almost forgotten how fine they feel. I hope I don't make them run. My hands are so rough. Oh, I'm gonna go try them on right now." She left and came back wearing the stockings and twisted around to see if her seams were straight in the back. "This is pure vanity. But I'm going to take them off and save them for some place nice." She put them back in their box. "You are so sweet but you really shouldn't have." She gave Daddy a kiss. "But I'm glad you did."

"Don't you go saving them till they dry rot. Figure out some place nice to go and we'll go."

Bay had been making a long boat out of newspaper and was looking for a pen to initial it with. "Daddy can I use your pen?"

"Yes, but why?"

"I want to initial the ship I just made."

"Okay. But give it right back."

When he was done he handed Daddy his pen then came in the living room and put the paper ship on the floor. "This is a Japanese ship. Let's bomb it."

So we all began to stomp it and make crashing noises. Daddy came in.

"Here now behave! What are y'all doing?" He picked up the crushed paper.

"That's a Japanese ship and we're bombing it. See the J.P. on its side?"

Daddy looked. "Well, what does the P stand for?"

"Panese," Bay said. "Jap-Panese."

Daddy plopped down on the couch laughing. "Oh, now I get it." He laughed again.

Then he went and showed the ship to Mother and they both laughed. Bay just thought they were pleased that we had bombed a Jap-Panese ship.

That night we wrote to our uncles overseas and Mother would put them in with her letters. To keep from wasting paper we all wrote a line or two on the same sheet. When Aunt Lucy or Grandma would write, Mother would use the backs of their letters to reply. But she saved our uncles' letters and tucked them in her keepsake box.

She especially valued this one that Uncle Edward sent where he told the story of how he and his company of soldiers, led by General George Patton, were going out on the front lines toward Germany. They rapidly advanced across France and toward West Germany. It had been bombed and was ready for them to secure for the allies. On their way the platoon came upon a whole battalion of Germans with tanks, jeeps and machine guns. They stood there frozen, ready to be blown into smithereens.

Then all of a sudden a glowing white bridge, with a line of angels walking over it singing the most beautiful song anyone had ever heard, came between them and the Germans. When the misty vision was gone so were the Germans.

They continued into the town and secured it without trouble. He ended the letter with the words of President Roosevelt, "The only thing we have to fear is fear itself."

Many times the two brothers had told Mother that they knew there would be danger and loss of life, but they never dreamed of miraculous interventions from God above. They said she shouldn't worry because everything was in God's hands.

Uncle Hank wrote that he was sending Christmas presents home for everyone and couldn't wait to tell her what he was sending her. A golden U.S. Navy pin to wear on her coat and he said, "I have it on good authority from the man upstairs that this war is going to be all right. No matter what happens we will meet again, either here or there. God's will be done. I love y'all."

Every night before prayers we stood together to quote a Bible verse and sing "God Bless America" or one of our patriotic songs. I thought the words to "Field of Artillery" were "Filler Tiller Ree." I sang out, "For it's hi, hi, he, in the filler tiller ree." I didn't know why I was singled out to sing some of these songs alone until Shelly told me what I was doing and why they wanted me to sing by myself sometimes.

"I thought it was because I knew all the words and sang it so well."

"I sing well and I know all the words. But do you see me standing by myself to sing?"

"I never thought about that."

"Obviously not. Just watch the next time they tell you to sing. They will be trying not to laugh. Go ahead, watch."

"No. I don't want to sing by myself anymore." I ran into the living room and joined in coloring with Zeke and Bay. They were coloring the funny paper of Nancy and Sluggo. I colored the Katzenjammer Kids.

The very next time I was asked to sing alone I said, "Not without everybody singing with me because I don't know the words by myself."

Shelly smiled at me and nodded.

Daddy had been sending payments to Mr. Roberts back home for the bill. One day he got a letter back that said the debt was cleared and that he was saving our place for us whenever we wanted to come back. He said other folks would have ran out on the debt. In appreciation he was giving Daddy our old cabin and its plot of land. But we couldn't leave this confined secret city right now. Daddy's work wasn't finnished.

Christmas passed and the New Year came. It was now 1945 and we were still a world with no peace. It was hard to believe that it had been over three years since we all stood under the great tree of lights on that first Christmas of the war.

Mother was sewing and asked me to go get her the scissors. When I reached out for them I saw two pairs. I fumbled around till I got a good hold on the scissors. Then my vision cleared. I told Mother that there were two pairs, and one went away. Mother put her hand on my forehead to see if I had fever.

"Do you feel sick?" she asked.

"No," I answered.

"Okay. It just happens sometimes for no reason."

I went back to coloring. As I did the lines blurred and I couldn't color right. I put my crayon down and started crying. "I can't color! The lines are too blurry!"

Mother laid her sewing down and came over to me.

"Close your eyes for a minute and then try looking again."

I did, but when I opened them the lines were still blurry.

Mother hugged me and told me it would be all right. "This happens to people all the time Clair, but it goes away. It's going to be all right."

She put me in bed to rest with a cool rag on my head.

Later she and Daddy took me to see an eye doctor. He checked my eyes and gave them some drops that felt like coals of fire. It hurt every part of my head when Daddy would drop them in. They had to hold me down while I kicked and screamed and closed my eyes tight to keep the drops of hell's fire out. But they always seemed to get in.

One morning Mother came in where I was sleeping and I couldn't get up I was so sick. I hurt all over my body and I didn't want to move.

Mother and Daddy took me to the hospital where a black man came out and carried me in. He put me in a room with a glass in it where I could look over at the girl in the next room. No one could come in without masks.

A few days passed and I started to feel better and people didn't have to wear the masks anymore when they came to see me, but everyone who came to see the girl in the next room still did. I had lost the sight in my left eye but I was feeling better and I wasn't seeing double anymore.

One day my nurse came in and stood at the foot of my bed. "Carrie, did you take your medicine?"

I lay still not saying a word.

"Carrie, did you take your medicine?"

I lay staring at her.

She came over and took my arm and shook me. "Did you take your medicine?"

I shook my head and said quietly, "Yes, ma'am."

"Why didn't you answer me?" the nurse asked.

"My name isn't Carrie," I said.

The nurse walked out laughing. I looked at the girl in the next room. She lay still and quiet. She must be Carrie. I wished that she wouldn't sleep all the time so we could wave to each other and I wouldn't feel alone.

Finally, the day came that I was to go home. I was so happy to get back and see Shelly, Zeke, Bay and my Matilda doll.

When I arrived there was a letter from Maxine waiting. No one had opened it till I got home so we could all read it together.

She wrote, "Y'all won't believe it. We'd tried everything we could think of to help James. Nothing worked. One day James said he wanted fried chicken for supper. So Mama ran out and got her fattest hen and fried it up for him. By the time she had got it all done and took it to him he didn't want it no more. Said it took too long. He threw the plate at her. I got mad and went out in the yard and caught a chicken then took it in there and threw it on his head. I told him the next time he wanted chicken to go get it and fix it for his own lazy good for nothing behind. When I threw that thing it went into a squawking fit and danced on his head clawing and flapping its wings.

"James jumped out of bed and fell onto the wheelchair. It sent him and the chicken rolling across the room. I looked at him in fear for my life as he lay on that floor but he just sat up and looked at me. I put both my hands on my hips and looked right back and asked him what he was going to do about that? I called him some names and told him I could do anything I wanted now and he couldn't do nothing about it 'cause he was so pitiful and crippled. James was stunned for a second before he let out one of his rip-roaring laughs. He laughed and laughed and now he's just as much like James as ever. He said to tell y'all hey and he sure misses everyone. I do, too. I hope everything is good with y'all. Write me back soon."

We were all so happy to hear about James.

Chapter Fifteen

A Fearful Secret

THE voice of President Roosevelt blared over the radio again, telling us that the Germans and Japanese were fighting like pure fanatics but that they'd never be able to win. Ultimate victory for the allies was certain. He said, "The American people must not relax their efforts to produce weapons of war."

It was coming up on spring now. What we didn't know was how very ill our President was. From his strong voice coming through the radio he sounded well. Roosevelt pushed himself beyond his total endurance to work toward building an alliance between these four big allied leaders. He put his hopes in the nations uniting to prevent there ever being another war on this planet. He worked hard and his polio-weakened body left him tired and ill.

On April 12, 1945, he died of a cerebral hemorrhage. All America mourned this dedicated leader as the Vice President, Harry Truman, took the oath of office and became our new President.

With the death of Roosevelt came a cloud of sorrow and uneasiness. But we would press on in his memory. We would do all we could to honor this great man's legacy.

With the spring the mountains and valleys of Oak Ridge came alive with color. Where once only dirt and mud resided, lush green grass sprang up and wild flowers speckled the landscape. Even in the middle of war, sorrow and terror, life flourished again.

Today was Saturday. Mother and Daddy were taking us to the picture show to see Roy Rodgers. I always wanted to be like him. I loved the action and adventure. I had begged Mother for a pair of pants and she bought me a pair of girl's slacks. I was so disappointed. I wanted a pair of jeans like Zeke and Bay wore. Today my skirt-tails wouldn't bother me, I was going to see Roy beat the bad guys!

We walked into the dark room and the large screen stood tall in front of me. Daddy went to buy popcorn and drinks while we found a good seat. Bay fidgeted with excitement. "Sit still." Mother told him. Suddenly the lights dimmed as the screen lit up and America the Beautiful began to play. After that came the reports on the war and praise for our committed troops and hardworking American citizens. Tanks rolled across the screen, soldiers marched, American flags waved. A 'Popeye the Sailor Man' cartoon was followed by the opening credits for the brave and noble Roy Rodgers' movie.

I chomped eagerly on my pop corn as Roy Rodgers whipped all the bad guys without even loosing his gleaming white hat!

We left the theater and night had already fallen. Before we'd gotten outside good, an air raid siren wailed. We turned and ran back toward the building just as the lights everywhere went out. We were in pitch black darkness. I felt like it was smothering me, I couldn't breath. When all over the night sky bright lights began to flicker. I thought this was it...the end of the world I'd heard so much about. Once inside the building we sat waiting. Would we get an all clear again? Everyone quietly waited. Finally when the all clear did come, we mulled around talking about the strange light display. No one knew what it was, and we were never told.

Not long afterward Daddy came home from the war plant upset. He was near tears and shaking. "We have been making an atomic bomb," he told Mother. "Today it was pulled out and readied for testing. I am so afraid because none of us know what it will do."

"Atomic? What in the world is that? Why didn't you tell me before?" Mother asked.

"None of us knew what we were making. They're taking it to Mexico to test it. We thought we were making batteries and ammunition. We were making energy for what they call an atomic bomb. Something to do with splitting atoms. I feel like this will either end the war or the entire world." For the first time in my life, I saw my Daddy cry. Mother hugged him.

When we went to bed that evening I noticed the wind picking up and a far rumbling sound of thunder. The curtains slowly ballooned from the raised window as they filled with the cooling wind that took the sting out of this hot summer night. A sharp, bright flicker of lightning x-rayed through them. I curled up on my bed and listened to the soft whispering rain.

I thought about one of Shelly's poems,

The softest rain, like fingers came,
groping down my windowpane,
while swaying trees, against the eaves,
swept the walls with trembling leaves

As I drifted into a sweet sleep a loud crashing thunderbolt jarred me awake. Flashes of lightning lit the sky as I sat up in bed.

Soon Daddy was called to the plant because of the fierce weather. They were afraid that the storm might detonate the bomb. He had to crawl up on it and unscrew a cap or something. No one, not even our government, had any idea of the magnitude of this bomb. It could be a dud or it could wipe out all creation.

The testing was beyond their wildest imaginations. The deep purplish cloud could be seen for miles. They brought a film back to show the people the magnitude of destruction that the bomb caused. The film showed a man being absorbed so fast by the bomb's fierce winds that his shadow was left after he was gone. That was how fast anyone could be wiped off the face of the earth.

I heard Mother and Daddy talking about it.

"I didn't know what it was. I thought it was batteries I was working on," Daddy said.

"We could have all been killed! That thing could have wiped us all away! That's what happened to Clair, that's why she was so sick! It was the radiation. She must have been exposed to it somehow!"

"Now, Madge. Don't get carried away. Everyone's all right. We're all fine." Daddy held her close. "We all knew it was just a matter of time before somebody decided to use Einstein's theory of relativity."

"Uh-huh, sounds like you knew a little more about it than you let me know Mr. battery maker for the army."

"No, really, I didn't know! They just told a few of us the other day!"

"How could you work on the thing and not know?"

"We all just worked on parts. We had no idea!"

"And what about the danger we were in had the Germans found out what we were doing here? Now I know the reason for all this secrecy and blackouts!"

"Well, would you rather Hitler have taken over America too? He'd just about taken over the rest of the world! Don't forget, we're in a war here with evil. At least we have something to stop it with now. They say Hitler was working on building one too. Maybe even the Japs too! Could you imagine something like that in their hands? Praise God it's in America's hands."

Not long after we heard that America had dropped the atom bomb on Hiroshima. It was dropped on August 6, 1945, totally obliterating that area. Radios and newspapers gave the people employed within the area the first inkling of the true nature of Clinton Engineer Works. The town became a beehive of celebration and sharing of the first newspaper accounts with each other.

People shouted, horns honked, "The war is over now for sure!"

Yells of celebration echoed throughout the town.

Daddy came in bringing Mother this letter he had received, and it read:

ARMY SERVICE FORCES
United States Engineer Office
Manhattan District
Oak Ridge, Tennessee

6 August 1945

TO ALL MILITARY AND CIVILIAN PERSONNEL MANHATTAN DISTRICT.

1. *The war department has extended to all military and civilian personnel*

> *of the Manhattan District its hardiest congratulations for meritorious service preformed in producing the atomic bomb.*
>
> *2. Major General Leslie R. Groves has asked me to express to you the deep appreciation felt by the war department and by himself for the unselfish and untiring effort you have made and the magnificent results you have achieved.*
>
> *3. Our first objective has been reached. We must press on lest the Japs catch their breath. Remember, they are tenacious fighters and they have not yet quit. Let us produce with unslackening speed so that final victory can be won at the earliest possible moment.*
>
> *K. O. Nichols,*
> *Colonel, Corps of Engineers,*
> *District Engineer.*

By August 15, the Japanese had surrendered. Mrs. Ruby came running to our house with her paper still in hand. "Look Mrs. Brown! We're in the paper, Oak Ridge! We stopped those Japs! The war is over!"

The roadway was full of people from all parts of America who came to see where the atom bomb had been built. Yet they still could not get inside the gates. So they just parked overlooking the town.

Oak Ridge had been nonexistent to outside folks, but inside it was the *Manhattan Engineer District*, the camouflage name for the *Clinton Engineer Works*, which made the atom bomb. Only a select few knew about it. It was the hidden secret city and we lived, worked and played there.

Suddenly, a certain amount of pride swept over us all. This work had saved the world and we were a part of it. For days we basked in the glow. All Mother could think about was getting out of here as soon as possible.

The Japanese signed the surrender document on the ship USS Missouri right on Zeke's and my birthday, September 2, 1945. We were having a big party not only to celebrate our birthday but also the United States' victory.

Alexander, Judy and Julia, their folks, and even Granny One came to the celebration. As they helped Granny One into the house, her ninety-three-year-old feet sloshed over the floor like lonesome waves against a deserted beach. The cake was iced in red, white and blue with peppermint sticks for candles. We blew horns and threw confetti and celebrated till late that evening. Granny One kissed our cheeks, wished us a Happy Birthday and told Mother that kids were the highest calling in life and jewels in her crown. We liked being jewels. Maybe Zeke and I were star sapphires since we were born in September.

The end of the war had brought jubilant good feelings. Everyone basked in the peacefulness and security of a world finally Stilled. It was as if the mighty surging water rapids had found a quiet place. Everyone rejoiced in this fresh breath of peace. Now we could float on this calm, peaceful river called freedom and victory.

Daddy brought out his fiddle and rosined the bow. He swept it over the strings and the house was full of music. It felt like we were at one of the barn dances back home. Our souls soared on the notes that glided through the air and we danced as if our feet had wings.

It was the fall of 1945 when we returned to our simple cabin in the Mississippi Delta. We pulled up in front of the place in the old green truck. It wasn't nearly as magnificent as the Oak Ridge house, but it felt grand to me.

As I pushed open the misshapen door it squeaked from its rusty hinges. Spider webs quivered in the corners. Light blared through the chinked cracks and shocked the drabness of the small cabin. I was home.

I walked through the cabin and out the back door. I heard the sound of singing in the distance. I walked around the house to see who was coming. I recognized the song. It was Floyd's old song, but it wasn't Floyd's voice. This voice was deep and throaty...rather nice as it sang out, "Ca-Ca-Ca Clair-ee." I stared toward the tall manly figure that traipsed toward me. He was nearly as tall as James Stokes with hair the color of winter sage. It gently floundered in the soft breeze as he walked. A wayward sprig danced onto his forehead and rested in a curl above his right eye. "Hello, Clair." He smiled. The deep voice poured out over his full lips and gleaming white teeth that overlapped a bit in the front. "Floyd? Is that you?" I couldn't believe my own eyes.

"Yep, its me. I heard y'all was home and thought I'd drop by and see my girl. I have to say it, you're just as pretty as ever." He said as he shyly looked down and scrapped his boot in the dirt.

"Y-you sure have changed. You look different." I saw a kindness in his eyes and heard a gentleness in his voice that hadn't been there before. I felt the heat in my cheeks as I remembered how mean I'd treated him. This handsome, figure had replaced ol' fat bugger-lipped Floyd. His lips were a perfect fit for his face, his smile was pleasant and desirable. How could this be him? I'd only seen guys like this in the picture shows. I just stood there like a knot on a log wishing that the dry Delta dirt would swallow me up.

"You ain't still sore at me are you, Clair?" I didn't know what to say. How could I tell him that he was handsome and charming? Even his voice was wonderful...where did ol' Floyd go?

Mother called me, "Clair! Come on now and help us!"

"I've got to go." I said. "I've got to go help."

"Okay, I'll see you around." He smiled. "You're still my girl, you know." This time I didn't rebuke him.

I walked back to the truck where everyone worked at unloading it. As I reached to lift a box, I heard a small coo and turned to see the purest white dove fluttering in the blue Delta sky. I pointed without saying a word and Mother looked. "It's a dove, Clair, God's bird."

We all stood on the dry dirt in front of the cabin hugging one another and watching as it flew out of sight.

"It's the bird of peace, Mother. Sometimes there's a dove!"

Author's Postscript

"Sometimes There's A Dove" was inspired by my Mother's stories about her life as the daughter of a poor half Native American sharecropper in Mississippi and living within the gates of Oak Ridge Tennessee during WWII. This fiction is based on truth. Clair, the main character, has been drawn from my idea of what my Mother must have been like as a little girl: soft hearted, trusting, honest and truthful. Sometimes a tomboy, she could stand up for herself if provoked.

I was sixteen years old when I wrote the first draft of this novel. It went through many changes and names over the coming years. "The Ghost Train," "The Third Trestle," "Life In The Delta," and finally "Sometimes There's a Dove." I was offered two contracts for the novel. The first was in 1990 the second in 1994 but I wasn't happy with either of them.

1995 was a hard year for me and my family. My sister lost a baby, my Grandmother died in June and my Grandfather followed her in August. It took me five more years to start writing again. I rewrote this novel for the last time in the spring of 2001.

I was looking on the Internet for publishers when 'Twilight Times' caught my eye. I sent an inquiry to the publisher, Lida. After reading the first chapter and synopsis, she asked for the rest of the novel.

I would have to type it up again before sending it. While I was going through this process September 11th of 2001 came and I was glued to the news. I didn't want to work on this novel about WWII when we had been hurt so bad. I felt as if I had been punched in the gut. All of my drive and ambition was wiped out.

As our leaders pleaded with the American people to 'get back to normal' I wondered if anything could be 'normal' ever again, yet I tried. Because of this horrific event I recalled, that when I was trying to write about WWII for "Sometimes There's A Dove," I had made myself forget that I knew what the outcome was. I just put myself in the place of a regular person in the 1940's to better understand the thoughts and feelings of that time. Suddenly a wave of fear had overwhelmed me. I quickly stopped the research. I was glad I could come back to this time of peace.... knowing the outcome of WWII. I hoped the world would never have to go through anything like that again. Now, here I was living this fear that I had tried to write about...pretend to live in. Yet in real time I didn't secretly know the outcome of 9-11-01 and still don't. I didn't want to write about war right then and didn't suppose anyone wanted to read about it.

A few weeks later the encouraging point behind this novel hit me. War and evil do come, but so does peace and good. We must all continue to live and work for peace. I don't believe there's ever been a time when the whole world was at peace. But we must hold on to the hope that we humans will eventually find a way to live peaceably with each other. Until then, we'll look forward to the coming of the Dove. To the coming of peace...*Sometimes There's A Dove*...Sometimes There's Peace...

The next few days I worked nonstop until the novel was ready and sent it in. To my great joy it was accepted. Thank you for reading this novel. My hope is that it gives a bit more encouragement, strength, and hope to all.

Peace be with you,
Sincerely,
Cynthia Ward...

Author Bio

Cynthia Ward is a self-taught Mississippi artist and writer who overcame the stigma of a learning challenge called dyslexia. She went into the field of writing and challenged all the doubts, thus making a statement of the undaunting spirit and never ceasing ability to be successful by holding fast to one's dreams.

Keeping in mind the motto of her Mother, "How can you fail if you never quit?" Cynthia faithfully stayed in the race and now has had her debut novel, "Sometimes There's a Dove," published by Twilight Times Books.

Using this topic to reach out to others, Cynthia criss-crosses her home state of Mississippi giving motivational speeches at various education centers, conventions, colleges and libraries.

Ms. Ward is a reviewer for KnowBetter.com and E-Book Reviews Weekly. She has served as a judge for literary competitions and is EPIC coordinator for her state.

Currently she is working on her second novel; an historical mainstream, "By Way of the Rose."

Order Form

Don't miss any of these other exciting mainstream novels.

- Death to the Centurion (1-931201-26-9, $16.95 US)
- Jerome and the Seraph (1-931201-54-4, $15.50 US)
- Unraveled (1-931201-11-0, $15.50 US)
- WolfPointe (1-931201-08-0, $15.50 US)

Twilight Times Books
Kingsport, Tennessee

Mail Order Form

If not available from your local bookseller or favorite online bookstore, send this coupon and a check or money order for the retail price plus $3.50 s&h to Twilight Times Books, Dept. FD604 POB 3340 Kingsport TN 37664. Delivery may take up to four weeks.

Name: ______________________________

Address: ____________________________

____

Email: ______________________________

I have enclosed a check or money order in the amount of

$___________

for _____________________________________ .

If you enjoyed this book, please post a review at your favorite online bookstore.

Twilight Times Books
P O Box 3340
Kingsport, TN 37664
Phone/Fax: 423-323-0183
www.twilighttimesbooks.com/

Appendix

Book cover design by Laurie Burke.

Cabin photo by Dorothea Lange.
Library of Congress, Prints & Photographs Division, FSA-OWI Collection, [reproduction number, e.g., LC-USF34-018078]
Digital ID: fsa 8b38293

Dove by Judith Huey.